IT STARTED WITH A KISS

SHORT STORIES AND REFLECTIONS

WRITTEN AND COMPILED BY
RENEE´ FLEMINGS

COPYRIGHT © 2019

Reneesance Publishing

TABLE OF CONTENTS

THANK YOU & ACKNOWLEDGEMENTS

Thank you to Lynda Crawford for always being in my corner, being a guiding soul and mentor. Thank you to the all the interviewees, who shall remain anonymous or under their non de plumes as they asked when I began this process. Thanks to Laura Johnston, Marcus Scott, Salvatore Carolei and Kathleen Murray, the tasters of the Cocktails For Kissers, it was fun wasn't it? Thanks to my husband, Salvatore, your support is all. Finally, thank you to the kisses that I have had and remember, good, bad, and just plain weird, without them we would never have stories to tell.

If you are just open to the rhythm of the kiss you can just shift into their rhythm because you can tell. You have to listen to the kiss. Kisses have ears and kisses have messages and you have to listen to the kiss. (Interview with DC)

INTRODUCTION

When I first had the idea to write about kisses I considered it a silly, fun thing to do. However, as I began to interview different people I realized that there was more weight to it than I had originally anticipated. Many of the people I interviewed were at first curious as to why I wanted to talk about kissing and then they really began to connect with the idea and shared how important it is to them.

Why did I want to write about this? I noticed that several of the couples that I knew didn't kiss anymore. Which made the ones that I did see kissing seem unique. I wondered if people just stopped kissing at some point in a relationship, or if at some point it was unnecessary in a long-term relationship. I refused to believe that was true. As I began to interview people I began to have hope that kissing was still important no matter the age and that it still meant a lot and maybe I'm not just some hopeless romantic. I found the interviews to be funny, poignant and sometimes sobering. I conducted many of these interviews a very long time ago and put them aside because I wasn't sure of what I was going to do with them or how they would figure into this book. I knew the book would be short stories but how they would tie together I didn't have a clue and to be honest the idea scared me to death. I write plays. I write songs. Short stories intimidated me. So the whole project languished on a metaphorical shelf on my laptop.

Flash forward years later and I decided it was time to

take it off the shelf and make that leap. What I found to be interesting is I hadn't listened to or read the interviews for years before beginning writing the stories. I dove in and started writing and then went back to edit the interviews and discovered that many of the same perspectives and ideas were expressed in the interviews and for me spoke to a universality of thought, desire and longing around kissing.

   I hope you enjoy this book. I also hope that you kiss more, and you enjoy it!

HOW IMPORTANT IS KISSING OR A KISS?

Extremely important. I don't think I could be in anything with anybody that didn't have great kissing. To me the kiss is the gateway. There are two things that are gateways to me: A kiss and a conversation. I don't think either one is less important than the other because they both tell you everything you want to know. (D.C.)

I think in some ways it can be even more intimate than sex at least to me. There've been times when I've made out for hours, kissing and not having sex and I've felt very satisfied and happy. I was seeing a guy for a while, not a long while. He'd be getting ready to leave and he'd be like see you later—and (peck kissing) and I'd be like "Aww". I wanted a big good-bye kiss. I love kissing. (CAT)

It's at the very top, or the bottom because you can call it the foundation. It's, to me, it's more intimate than [sex] with somebody. I'm not sure why but for some reason the kiss has always held this ideology or it's a symbol of the heart. It can be hot, it can be passionate, to me it is the core. Sometimes I don't need more than that to feel intimately close to someone. To me a kiss and laughter. When I share laughter with someone I feel very intimate with them. Those are the closest moments. Sexually the other stuff is there, but it's not as important. (VB)

In The Dust

Neicey walked down the familiar street. Nothing had changed much in the five years since she's been kidnapped to the cold, remote world of Illinois from the Louisville she still loved and would always think of as home. Okay, so she hadn't really been kidnapped; she just liked to think of it that way since she hadn't even known where Illinois was back when she was twelve and her mother had said they were moving there to start over. The air smelled the same this June as it always had every summer she could recall in her fifteen years visiting or living here in the "Ville." In the heat of the city you could smell the flavor of the west end: the barbecue, the cigarettes, the remnants from some cheap liquor bottle discarded during a good night of partying that had likely gracefully flowed into the morning hours. That's how we party in the 'Ville she thought. It was nineteen seventy- two.

She'd just left from a visit with her former next-door neighbors. Mrs. Turner had remarked more than once how much Neicey had changed. She'd stared hard at her when she opened the door,

"Yes?" she'd asked with an edge to her voice.

"Hey Mrs. Turner, how you doin'?"

"Neicey? Girl look at you! You look all grown up now. Come on in here."

Neicey had followed her into the house for a conversation updating her on all the changes. Mrs. Turner and her husband Mark had divorced, like Neicey's parents. This was the weekend when Kitty, Mrs. Turner's daughter and Neicey's best friend from back in the day, and her annoying older brother Ray were visiting with their daddy. So, she missed them on this trip. It was funny how often Mrs. Turner kept coming back to how much Neicey had "got grown," as she called it.

This wasn't news to Neicey, but she didn't know how to explain it. She was fifteen and up until seemingly a few weeks ago she had the slight, bony figure of a boy. In fact, for many years she'd constantly had to remind people that she was a girl. Not anymore. She had gone from an AA cup to a B cup bra, from wearing boy's jeans to having hips that bordered on being full like her own mother's and a small waist. None of this was lost on Mrs. Turner or her mother.

When Neicey's mother came to visit her during her summer down in Louisville last month the first thing she did was ask, "What the hell have you been doin' down here?"

"What Mama?"

"Your boobs! And you've got hips!"

"I don't know. It just kinda happened. Maybe I don't know, maybe it's the humidity down here?"

"We're going to have to go shopping before I go back to Illinois." She seemed exasperated. "What have you doing?" she asked more insistently.

"Nothin' Mama."

She had no idea what her mother thought she could have done to make her body change. But, she had noticed that her old jeans didn't fit over her hips anymore and she had popped the buttons off two of the blouses she'd packed before leaving Illinois, so she'd started wearing a T-shirt underneath and leaving them open. At first it was embarrassing and annoying to feel so uncomfortable in her clothes, especially her favorite pair of jeans. However, the past week or two she'd also noticed that boys were looking at her differently, and one or two of the boys in her grandma's neighborhood asked to walk her home or would call her over for nothing. They didn't want to race or arm wrestle with her anymore because they knew she liked a good challenge--Neicey prided herself on being just as strong and tough as any boy. She also noticed they'd stopped talking about other girls in front of her like they used to before she... well, she guessed she could say she was pubering and wasn't sure what all was going to happen, but it was a change.

As she walked down the street she had to admit she really did like the looks she was getting although the new nicknames were weird to her, like "Loose Booty" --that one was kind of gross, but not as bad as "Juicy," which she hated. She'd heard older girls called names like that and worse before. She always cussed out any boy who talked nasty like that to her. Maybe she had pubered her way into a new level of being a girl. She didn't do it on purpose. She wasn't a woman, she knew that, but she was getting close and ol' Jessica King back in Illinois wouldn't be able to call her "Ironing Board Chest" anymore when they were changing for gym class.

Neicey caught her reflection in a drugstore window and stopped for a minute, pretending to look at the dolls, cough medicine, and candy display, when she was really admiring the way her turquoise and white hip-huggers really did hug her hips, and the white, midriff-baring top glanced above her navel so her flat stomach was visible when she moved just the right way. The white of the top highlighted the deep red brown color of her skin, and her hair was permed to lay down, with curls she could flip it whenever she wanted. Although Neicey was determined not to turn into one of those girls who'd flip their hair and giggle stupidly at the what the boys said. That was just ridiculous. Since she had been in the boy's club for so long, because they never thought of her as a girl, she'd heard them talk disparagingly about girls like that and she thought it was stupid to flip your hair for attention anyway. Stupid girls.

"Not me," She told her reflection.

She applied another layer of clear lip gloss. This whole "grown girl thing" was new and she realized that she was curious about what else it would bring into her world.

Neicey continued walking down the street, feeling the sun kissing her all over the bare skin of her arms, belly, the small space on her back that was still covered in peach fuzz. She began to swing her hips just a little bit; this is why Bradley Foster called her "Loose Booty," and it had stuck even though she'd told him to stop. She might have to punch him in the face next time he did it.

"I don't like that name, but I do like the way it feels to move my body like this," she thought.

She realized that during her wandering and reminiscing around her old neighborhood she'd ended up in front of Butchie Brown's house.

In that moment she was hoping Butchie Brown was around so he could see the new her. What would Butchie Brown have to say now?

She realized that the crush she'd had on Butchie Brown was just as strong as it was before she'd left Louisville and the thought of him still took her breath away.

Neicey stood there and pretended to dig through her purse when she was actually hoping he'd come out on his porch like he often did when she had lived in the neighborhood. This time she didn't want to race him; she couldn't run if she wanted to in the platform shoes she was wearing. He'd always won anyway. Butchie Brown was the only boy in her old neighborhood who could beat her in a race. Always, try as hard as she might, he'd reached the corner before her. She remembered the last time they'd raced, when she was thirteen and she thought her ribs would crack from having to breathe so hard to try keeping up with him. When they'd finished racing that last time, she stood there dripping sweat. Her face was blotchy red, and her muscles ached. She had run hard, slamming into the pavement, lifting her knees high, determined just once to beat him, even though he was two years older than her. She remembered thinking she really needed to beat him just this one time before moving away so she could "leave in him the dust," like he called it, in order to have him respect her instead of rubbing her head and saying, "You ain't never gonna beat me kid. You just a girl." Every time he said it, she felt her blood boil.

"One day Butchie Brown, I'm gonna beat you. You just wait. You gonna see!"
And he'd laughed and walked away shouting back at her.

"Never!"

Butchie Brown wasn't brown at all, he was black as midnight,

black like the velvet in her favorite top she got for Christmas one year.
His eyes were dark brown and fringed with the longest damn lashes
she'd ever seen on a boy. He was lean and you could see every muscle
rippling in his legs and arms as he pumped them hard when they raced.
He never seemed to have to breathe hard or sweat or anything. He was
just Butchie Brown. Beautiful Butchie Brown.

Neicey realized that she was feeling something a little different in
the pit of her stomach as she thought about Butchie in that moment and
it had nothing to do with racing. Except, well maybe her heart was
racing.

She stood there for the longest time wishing he'd come outside.

Suddenly the door opened slightly.

"Crap!" Neicey muttered and tried to figure out which way to
walk so as not to seem like she was doing exactly what she was doing,
waiting to see Butchie.

A bandana clad head poked out the door. A wiry, dark-skinned
woman, though she wasn't as dark as Butchie, of about sixty, peered at
Neicey though black rimmed glasses.

"What y'all want?"

"Oh! Hey Miss Brown. How you doin'?"

"Who're you?"

"It's me Neicey, from down the block."

"Oh, hey honey, how you doin'? You move back down here? I thought you was up north somewhere."

"Yes Mam. I'm still up in Illinois."

Since she was caught Neicey figured she may as well take the leap, so she moved up the steps to the porch.

"I'm down here visiting my family for the summer. Staying with my grandma."

"Well, that's nice."

"So how you doin', Miss Brown?"

"Oh, sweetie, I'm doing well as be as expected. Still kickin' but not high."

"That's what my grandma says sometimes. How's Butchie doing?"

"He's alright. I can't ever keep up with him. He runs the streets all the time. He's liable to be home round nine, ten o'clock, or maybe

not till the mornin'. Can't ever tell with him. You want me to tell him you

come by?"

"That's alright. Maybe I'll catch him next time. Thank you,

Ma'am."

"Alright now. Nice to see you. I've gotta go it's almost time for

my stories. You growed up, didn't you?"

"I guess. That's what my mama says."

"Well you be careful out there. Be good." With that she closed

the door.

Neicey was wondering why is she telling me to be careful and to

be good? I'm always good. Then she remembered a line from a Mae

West movie she watched a few months ago that always made her laugh,

"I'm always good, but when I'm bad I'm better."

She was thinking about that line and the Mae West movie while

she started walking toward the bus stop to head back to her

grandmother's house. She was disappointed. She wasn't sure exactly

why she was so disappointed. Yeah, she wanted to see Butchie, but she couldn't say what she was hoping would happen. Maybe she just wanted him to see her and say, "Well, you ain't a little girl anymore." She smiled as she thought about that, how cool that would be, when she heard her name.

"Neicey? Hey! Neicey is that you?"

Neicey turned to find Butchie Brown standing right behind her. The light behind him enveloping him in a halo of gold. She realized that she wasn't breathing. Oh, dear God, but he was beautiful.

"Neicey girl. Look at you!"

"Hey Butchie. How you doin'?"

"I'm good. You look like you're doing better than that."

She felt herself blush, dammit.

"I'm alright."

"What you doing down here?"

"Visiting my grandma for the summer. What you doing?"

"Just playing some ball."

Which made sense--he was holding a basketball in one hand. That's when she noticed the glistening sweat on his skin. She almost stopped breathing again when she paid attention to the fact that he was wearing a tank top and his muscles were even more defined than she remembered. He started to bounce the ball and with each bounce the flex in his biceps made her a little dizzy.

"You still trying to outrun the boys?"

"I don't race anymore."

"Oh yeah? So, I guess you ready to get caught now?" and he laughed.

"Got nothin' to do with you, cause you still can't catch me."

"You got those shoes on, otherwise, I'd give you a race. You know ain't nothin' changed, I can still outrun you." Then he smiled like they were sharing some kind of secret and her heart flip-flopped.

Neicey thought, "Oh my goodness, I am going to pass out if he does that again." She began to think it wasn't such a good idea to try to see him.

Her thoughts were interrupted by him throwing a casual arm around her. She nearly jumped out of her skin.

"Why you so jumpy? We used to always walk around like this,

remember?"

"Yeah, I remember."

"C'mon, walk with me a ways."

"Where?"

"Just walk with me. I wanna talk to you."

Her mind was screaming—Butchie Brown wants to TALK TO ME!!! Her crush for years was finally wanting to talk to her. Now her mind was racing. Did he just want to talk, or want to "talk," which is what everybody called it in The 'Ville when a boy and girl were sort of a couple? She was thinking it was a good thing she'd put her turquoise and white plaid pants on because they accentuated that she had hips and was growing up, which was good if you wanted to "talk" to someone.

"What you wanna talk to me about?"

"Something private."

"Like what?"

"Girl, come on now. I just wanna talk to you. Walk me home."

"Ain't that a switch? Hmmph."

"Oh, you growed up and now you all sassy and whatnot?" and he laughed again.

His laugh was like what she imagined the ocean would sound like when she finally got a chance to see it. It was like gentle thunder, but it shook her like loud thunder echoing against the earth, shaking everything it came into contact with. She walked with him.

As they approached the corner. He gently nudged her between two of the corner buildings. Her heart was beating so fast, she felt like a blade of grass being whipped around by the wind. She was hoping that she wasn't trembling outside as much as she was inside, so he'd notice.

"You know I always liked that you tried to beat me. Told me you had heart."

He turned to face her, looking deeply into her eyes.

Neicey was trying not to have a conniption. She felt like this might be it. He might actually kiss her. This was better than she had ever imagined. It was more than she'd ever fantasized about Butchie Brown back when she was a kid. This was before she'd been kissed by this boy in Illinois and that kiss was alright. It was sweet. Not much more than that but it was nice enough that they'd kissed a few other times. Then they'd just stopped kissing and she really didn't miss it. Now she realized that that was what she had wanted for all these years-- to kiss Butchie Brown, she wanted Butchie Brown to kiss her. Yes! This was it. She began to remember how she used to think about how soft his lips had to be; how sweet his breath would taste. How tender she knew it would be. And it was going to happen. She knew it-- she could just feel it and he knew it too. She could tell. She tried to work up some spit in her mouth so it wouldn't be dry and nasty tasting. Damn, why didn't she put that peppermint in her mouth?

Butchie looked at her funny. "You alright?"

"What? Oh, yeah—just uhmmm, had a catch in my throat."

When next he spoke, his voice was soft and had a different tone; it was a mellow trumpet on one of her Miles Davis albums. "Look at you all grown up now. How old are you?"

"Fifteen. I'll be sixteen in the fall."

"Damn, fifteen. Time moves fast. I'm eighteen now. So, am I too old for you?"

"Huh? What?"

"I'm thinking we know each other, been knowing each other for a long time, and maybe we could start talking. At least while you're down here. If you want?"

Neicey almost broke out in a happy dance and screamed YES!!! Instead, she was cool.

"I don't know. Maybe."

"Listen to you! 'Maybe.' You a mess girl."

"Yeah, I am, but when I'm bad I'm better." That wasn't quite how she wanted that to come out. It had sounded better when Mae said it in the movie.

"What?"

"Nothin'"

He looked at her for a long moment.

All she could focus on is HE'S GOING TO DO IT! WE'RE GOING TO KISS. FINALLLY. She licked her lips like she'd seen the girls in the hallway at school do when they were about to kiss their boyfriends. Butchie smiled then and it was a different smile than she'd ever seen on him before and she liked it.

"Maybe we could try? If you want."

After a pause, which sounded like she was trying to be cool, but in reality Neicey was trying to keep from shouting so it would come out sounding like she was in control. "Yeah. Okay. We can try." All while she was thinking, "YES!!"

"Okay then. I like that." And he gently stroked her cheek. "Damn, you sure are fine, and your skin is so soft."

Suddenly, they were both quiet and there was no sound. The traffic on busy Main Street was blanketed in silence. Everything else in the space around them vanished. It was if someone had made all the world a watercolor and she and Butchie Brown were the only objects that stood out in absolute relief. It made her think of one of those paintings they studied in Miss Triola's art class. She could feel her heart pounding against her ribs, harder than anytime she'd raced Butchie, harder than when she'd scored a home run in kickball, harder than when she'd set up scores for volleyball. Harder than when she'd won any kind of a sports tournament.

His hand moved behind her head and she let the weight of it fall so he could support it. He smiled.

She smiled.

As he began to move closer to her, she closed her eyes in preparation. She felt his gentle nibble on her lips, and she smiled. He moved to one side and then the other of her lips to kiss her gently.

She sighed and smiled.

"You like that huh?"

"Uhhh-hmmm." She breathed in and thought, "Oh God, yes, finally."

His lips connected to hers and his tongue gently prodded her, all he needed was gentle pressure as she opened her mouth slightly to allow his tongue in. Then they were kissing upper lips, lower lips in a paroxysm of sweetness. Then there was a new sensation.

Neicey suddenly felt as if her face was in a vacuum. He was sucking her lips into his mouth. There was panic. "What is this?" she wanted to ask, but she couldn't, as the whole lower portion of her face was being sucked into his mouth. She was afraid of what would happen if he didn't stop. It felt like being sucked into some deep space hole, like on Star Trek! Her fear and confusion continued as he began to suck her face into his mouth up to her nose and she couldn't breathe.

SUFFOCATION BY KISS!!

She tried to free herself, but the more she tried to move away the more he acted as though he thought she was saying she enjoyed this. She began to slap him on the back, and he began to moan. How he could make any sounds with his mouth full of her face she didn't know.

"Oooohhh yeeeeaaah," he moaned.

No, no this isn't how it was supposed to be. It was supposed to be soft, tender kisses, tongues exploring, passion, but this wasn't passion it was what she imagined kissing a plunger would feel like.

She used all of her force to push away from him, which released a gigantic "Thwwwaaaap!!!" sound. Her face around her mouth felt like she'd been scrubbing it with a steel wool pad and IT WAS WET! Her face from nose to chin was soaked with Butchie Brown's saliva.

Neicey stood there confused. Obviously Butchie Brown was too, because he was looking at her with furrowed brows.

"What?"

"N-n-nothin'."

"Something wrong?"

"No, oh no. I've just remembered that I've got to go. I told my grandma I'd be home about now, so I better catch the next bus."

"Aw man, I thought maybe we could go talk a little while."

"I've really got to go" Neicey said, fighting the impulse to dig in her purse for a napkin.

All she could think of was how badly she wanted some soap and water to fumigate her face.

"Okay, if you've really got to go. Hey, why don't you give me your number so I can call you? Maybe we can go out this weekend?"

"Yeah, sure. Seven seven four three six three seven." She rattled a fake number off, while trying to avoid the drip of his spit onto her clothes and refrain from wiping her chin on her sleeve. Couldn't he see the wet around her mouth that he'd left?

"Can you write it down for me?"

"I don't have a pencil. I have a good memory, give me yours and I'll call you tonight."

As he said his number, her mind was on the drug store across the street, hoping they had some Kleenex and rubbing alcohol to clean her face.

"You got it?"

"Yep. Call you tonight. I've gotta go before the bus comes."

"Can I get another kiss?"

"Really, can't! Sorry gotta go Butchie. Don't want my grandma to get mad at me. She'll ground me, then we won't be able to go out next weekend. Good to see you...talk to you tonight."

He smiled and his eyes twinkled as he said, "Alright, we don't wanna piss your grandma off. See you Friday?"

"Yep." Neicey was halfway to the corner, waiting to cross the street. She waved at him as he bounced the ball.

"Girl, you sure grew up!! Damn."

She smiled as she scooted across the street towards the drug store.

He called after her, "Don't you need the bus going the other way?!"

"Naw, my grandma moved she lives over this way now." She lied.

She waited until he walked off toward his home before she rushed into the drugstore. As she was collecting her purchases of mouth wash, rubbing alcohol, and Kleenex, she realized that she'd finally left Butchie Brown behind. It wasn't how she had expected or wanted, but she had left him in the dust.

What does a kiss tell you?

I wonder if that kinda tells you about their personality. This one guy I didn't like his kiss, it was aggressive, but he was not aggressive at all. He was very self-involved and wanted to satisfy his needs. I think a kiss tells you that they're not selfish. Just because you're in a relationship, you like someone—that you want to be intimate with this person—and not just sex. If someone is willing to really kiss you it's saying to me that they are willing to give me something of themselves. So they're willing to at least put some effort into the relationship.
Your kiss shows me something about your personality.

(CAT)

A good kiss tells you that something really right is going on in that moment. Really right. It's the power of now. That's what a really good kiss does. It places you in the NOW, it erases the past and it negates the future because it's right then and there. (DC)

Their level of respect or regard – like I'm not just going to grab your head and jam my tongue down your throat. It tells me how experienced they are, and I like that. Okay, they've been around long enough to know what a good kiss is --or not. It also just tells me if we're on a different page. [It] tells me how brave or open they are.

Because if it's important to someone, then it tells me how they approach a bond or a relationship.

There was a guy that I met on the subway, I was on my way home from a gig and we ended up starting to date. I really liked kissing him. We never got intimate beyond kissing. What was interesting was I felt like I really wanted to get to know him. Like we both—seemed to like that act—it was intimate, it was sweet, it was endearing, but I never felt the need to go beyond that. I almost felt like that was all I ever really needed to get from this. It was about three or four months we dated. So, it does tell me their values on a relationship. (VB)

Haiku #1

Tenderness of lips
Transformation moved to bliss
Waves explode on sand.

The Gift

Dim morning light slithered through the blinds barely caressing the golden walls of Edgar's room. He took a breath. It was staccato and shallow. At least it was a breath. He looked at the things on the table next to him. A photo. He was certain it was him and... Kate? No, Karen. No, that wasn't it. He realized it was going to be that kind of a day. Things floated around in his mind like phantoms. Ghostlike and shadowy, teasing him, frustrating him, eventually pissing him off. Edgar closed his eyes. Carleen. That was it. Carleen. Who was his... daughter? Yes. No. His wife?

Edgar kicked the covers off his lower body with difficulty, but he got them off. The first victory of the day. This was good. Last week he had tried kicking them and ended up on the floor and they had to come in and get him up. Those damned people who talked to him like he was a child. Yes, he forgot things and had trouble getting around, that's still no reason to treat him like a child. He'd been places dammit. He had lived and now he was old. That's what happened when you got to be his age, whatever the hell that was. He laid there and looked at the clock on the wall. They made sure it was a big clock, with big numbers, and it was whattayoucallit? Digital! It was insult to injury. He hadn't forgotten how to tell time. He just had trouble remembering some things. Yesterday it was that thing that was wooden and had the black hairs—no, bristles--on it. He didn't know how to use it and one of the them got upset cause he thought he was supposed to brush his teeth with it. It had brushes on it, you held it in your hand—it made sense to him dammit. He watched as the numbers shifted six times, while he breathed in and out. Edgar was preparing to face the day.

He pressed his shoulders into the almost too soft mattress below him, and with a strong exhale he raised his upper body to a sitting position. Next, he slowly shifted his legs over to the edge. He would've given himself the luxury of time if he was sure he had enough to spare. Time, the one thing that he had too much of on a daily basis and too little of in the grand scheme of things. "Grand scheme of things," a phrase he hadn't used since he was running his business and selling ad space, a lifetime ago. He looked down at his swollen feet, the blue veins showing against the almost translucent skin. Then he remembered: He had to pee. That's why he couldn't take his time. He didn't want them to put him in those damned diapers. He knew a lot of people on his floor wore the cursed things. One of the final humiliations. He thought about those commercials on the toaster, wait no, television and they'd try to make it seem like it's an everyday thing. Like it was a natural progression in life to start wearing diapers when you were a goddamned grown man. Women could do as they pleased, but a man shouldn't be wearing diapers especially if you'd worn the uniform of a baseball player, a naval officer, and then the Madison Avenue uniform of suit and tie for decades. They could say whatever the hell they wanted, but he couldn't abide with them trying to put a diaper on him. So, get up he must right now before he pissed himself and get up he would.

The urgency of his bladder said, "Move now." He pushed himself to standing and although he was slow, he was steady to the doorway. Steady to the bowl. He held onto the railing against the wall as he lifted the seat and took out his business to conduct his business. He waited.

"Goddammit," he muttered as he stood there, his Johnson in his hand, and nothing happened. Well, he would wait it out, cause he knew as soon as he crossed back to the bed he would have to start the whole damned process over again. "Goddammit," he said again.

As he shook his head in frustration he caught a glimpse of a reflection in the mirror. There was a woman standing by his bed. She looked familiar, sort of, maybe? Like they'd met long ago, but he couldn't remember where. Edgar looked over his shoulder, as best he could. He didn't want to turn too far and make a mess on the floor if the floodgates should open so they could come in here tsk, tsking and insist on him putting on the damn diaper or worse.

"Yeah?" he said gruffly.

She smiled at him.

"A little privacy here. Tryin' to handle my business, you don't mind," he said when she didn't respond.

The doors were hooked to a gadget on the wall so you couldn't lock yourself in. One of the other people on the floor had done that so she could try to cut her wrists open. Stupid broad, she tried to use a spoon she'd pilfered from the dining room. She was way gone man. Too far gone.

Edgar shifted his weight to block the view from the woman. He looked in the mirror again and she had turned her back.

"Thanks." He wasn't sure what the hell to do. The possibility of having an accident was still there, so here he was stuck with some strange broad in his room, nice looking broad, too, while he was holding onto his business. Well, he was sure it wasn't something she'd never seen before. She had that look about her. Worldly, been around, seen things. He was sure she'd seen a man's business before.

"Sorry, sometimes this takes a minute. I'll be right with ya," he growled at her.

Why doesn't she say something, he wondered?

After what seemed an eternity, a gentle flow began and then picked up speed. Sweet, sweet relief. After he flushed and turned on the water to wash his hands, he caught her reflection again and she smiled shyly at him.

"I know you?'

"Yeah. How you doin' Edgar?"

"Not so good with names these days." He walked slowly into the room.

She definitely looked like a broad who knew what she was doing. Her hair was a blend of blonde and red, shoulder length and wavy. Her eyes were dark, almost a violet blue and hypnotic, but it was her lips that caught Edgar's attention. Those lips were full, pouty, and lacquered a deep, deep red. He couldn't take his eyes off those lips.

"So, whattaya want? I don't have no services planned for today. I don't think anyway. Yesterday was the doctor's but that's it."

"Straight to it. I like that. You don't remember me?"

It was more than a question, it was a dare: say the wrong thing and you lose, Edgar. But lose what was what he wanted to know. He reached for the large print calendar on the nightstand and his wire-rimmed glasses. He scanned the dates.

"Say, what's the date?"

She just smiled at him.

"It's the twentieth ain't it? I think it is. Yesterday was... yeah, that's today. Monday. I got nothin' here.

She said nothing.

"You do look familiar. We met before, right? Where'd we meet? Sorry, things get foggy sometimes. They should call this place Foggy Arms or something like that." He huffed his dry laugh.

It was clear she wasn't going to give him any clues. Maybe she was some kind of doctor, or maybe she didn't mean him any good. Edgar started to wonder what kind of broad comes into a man's room, watches him pee, and then just sits and stares at him.

"It's almost time for breakfast, so you need to tell me what it is ya want. Is that it? You here to bring me down to breakfast? I told them I can get there by myself, dammit." When she said nothing, he kept going." Look, I apologize, I don't remember you—help me out here"

"How ya doing?"

"What?" He was caught off guard by that. Maybe she was some kind of nutjob came off of one of the other floors, but she looked way too young for that.

"How are you Edgar? Are they treating you okay here?"

"Same's they treat anybody, you know. So, where I know you from? Wait, are you a friend of Channy's?"

He was thinking about one of his buddies from the old neighborhood. Channy, the definition of a good guy, short, a mutt. He came from all kinds of stuff: Irish, Italian, and a little Puerto Rican he said sometimes. The two of them had gone on double dates a few times before he'd married… Carleen? He hadn't seen Channy in years, so he had no idea why his name came up out of the fog of his memory. That was grabbing at ash on water.

"Who?"

"Never mind."

"Who's Channy?"

"An old friend from long ago. Naw, you can't be a friend of his; you're too young. Way too young."

She smiled at this. "You're probably right. I'll tell you a secret, I'm older than I look." She stretched out her right leg languidly and crossed it over the left.

"Yeah? You're definitely too young though, to be one of Channy's friends. Tell ya I don't even know why I thought of him. I haven't thought of Channy in years, decades. He's a good one. Nice, stand-up guy. He…" His voice trailed off as a memory came to him.

"He what?" She leaned forward in the chair.

"Nothin', just… he died a long time ago. The Big C got him. I told him he needed to stop smokin', but he wouldn't. He just kept it up." He shook his head to clear his thoughts. "Look, I really gotta go Miss. You gotta tell me what ya want cause I don't want to miss breakfast. The oatmeal tastes like ass, but it's better than those dried up eggs, and if I don't get down there they stop serving breakfast, and then I don't get to eat until one o'clock." He laughed softly.

"What's so funny, Edgar?"

"I was just thinking how people say something tastes or smells like ass, but how do you know that—I mean what ass tastes like, ya know?" She leaned back, as if she'd been insulted. "Sorry, I probably shouldn't say something like that to a female and I just… it's not right. Sorry."

"That's one thing that hasn't changed, has it?"

"What?"

"Your sense of humor." She stood up and walked around the dismal room. She gently ran her hands over the cheap cotton window curtains, then trailed them along his dresser with the pictures and the two knick-knacks on top. He couldn't figure out what they were or who they were from. They were just things sitting there for no damn good reason.

"So, where'd you say we met?"

"I didn't. I'm kind of sad that you don't remember me, Eddie."

"I never said I didn't remember you. I just, you know I've always been bad with names, and like I said, I'm worse now."

"Oh. Is that all? You sure Eddie?"

"Eddie? Nobody's called me that in a long time."

She laughed. Sometimes people call a laugh throaty and deep; hers was like from-the-bottom-of-a-well deep. It was like going-down-a-coal-mine-after-a-blast kinda deep. His dad did that kind of thing before they moved to Brooklyn, working in coal mines. He was what? Nine, ten years old, and he remembered the blue Buick Daddy drove. Feeling like a marble bouncing around in that giant back seat. Where that came from he didn't know, but it made him smile and lose himself in that moment.

"Eddie, put your seat belt on honey," Mother would call back over the seat.

He'd roll all around that big back seat. He was the only kid. Some days he loved it; others he was lonely. He knew lonely. He'd been lonely most of his life, but he'd never own it to a soul. He liked the free and single life, that's what he'd say. Then he'd met… Isabel… no, Carleen and he was the happiest man alive. Carleen, so beautiful and kind. She wasn't the kind of broad that you thought about how good the lay was gonna be beforehand. That's like imagining that Mother Teresa broad naked and you didn't do that. It was always good. He remembered that about her. She was a great lover, a great friend. A great wife. What happened to her? He tried to remember.

"Eddie?" The voice snatched him back into the present. Into this room that held nothing for him aside from being a place to sleep and piss when he could. "You're being rude. Don'tcha want to talk to me?"

"I'm sorry, but I don't even know who you are. Am I supposed to know you?"

She smiled again and he again was mesmerized by the beauty of her lips, of her mouth. He could tell she could kiss. He could tell that she could kiss real good. The thought of that gave him a surprise he hadn't had in a while and he put his hand over his crotch so as not to embarrass himself. He even felt himself blush. She laughed from the depths of the earth again, but softly this time.

"Don't worry Eddie. It ain't something I never seen before."

She stood up and walked directly in front of him. Her nearness was a tender caress on his heart. She tilted her head to one side and regarded him with a crooked smile that made her lips all the more tantalizing.

"Oatmeal!" he shouted.

She laughed loudly. "What?"

"I gotta get down to breakfast, lady. Look, just tell me what you want—"

She knelt in front of him.

"I brought you a gift, Eddie."

"What kind of gift?"

"I bet you'll like it more than oatmeal."

She began to lean towards him. Was it his imagination or did he smell tangerines? Tangerines and strawberries. The scent was familiar and sent sparks through his brain like an electrical jolt. He was wondering why he didn't try to get away from her. Then on second thought, she was a gorgeous woman, she smelled good, and it's the first time in a long time blood was flowing to parts of his body that he hadn't thought about in a while. He liked it. He missed it, this feeling of being alive. More alive than he'd been in years, or at least since his daughters… what the hell were their names? Didn't matter, they'd put him in this place and left him alone. He'd slowly been disappearing. Every time he looked in the mirror he saw less and less of himself. He remembered less and less, and once the memories were gone what was left? A half shadow of a man in a mirror that couldn't see past the dark. So no, Eddie wasn't going to move. He didn't care if she was a nutjob. He felt alive.

"How ya feelin', Eddie?"

"Nice. Real nice." His voice was low and breathy.

She was only a few inches away from him now. Her face close to his. He could smell the tangerines and strawberries and something else, what was it? The ocean. Dear God, he hadn't thought about the ocean in so long. How he'd loved the ocean and the feeling of having to navigate the waves, the taste of the salt. He was so alive right now.

Her eyes weren't blue, they were violet with flecks of dark brown around them and fringed with long eyelashes like her hair, red and blonde. She was so beautiful; he almost couldn't breathe. He watched as she parted her lips. He couldn't believe this was happening to him! But he wanted it. He leaned forward and closed his eyes, waiting for the touch. Every cell in his body was longing for the connection. He knew it meant something more than just this kiss. It was truly a gift.

Soft… soft… soft.

He was falling, waves were pushing him to the sky and bringing him down again with a tender embrace. He was back in the Caribbean, swimming—just like he remembered when he was on a tour there while in the Navy. The waves would envelope you in a gentle touch, a kiss

upon the skin, then back up towards the heat of the sun. Her tongue

gently traced his lower lip and then tickled his tongue. She tasted like

tangerines and strawberries. He opened his mouth and welcomed her

tongue deeper into him. There they were together, back and forth, small

kisses and then tongue and--Eddie hadn't been kissed like this

since... Since...

The girl. The woman at the club that night.

He was on his way home from the war. He'd had a rough tour and

had gone out by himself as usual. He was still claiming to be a loner. Not

your buddy-buddy type like the rest of the guys in his unit. He could

count his friends on one hand, and he was good with that. He'd gone

out that night to escape the cheap hotel room where he'd been hiding

for the past week. He wasn't sure he was ready to go home to Carleen

and the kids. He wasn't sure he was the same man—or what kind of a

man he was anymore after all the things he'd seen and done. He didn't

want to bring half a man home to his family. So, he'd lied and said he

was being held up by paperwork and would be home as soon as he could. He knew if he couldn't get back in touch with the man he was before he'd been shipped overseas going home wasn't an option. They deserved better than a half-dead guy just trying to get by.

He went into this club The Raven's Nest. Jazz until ten, then rock and roll until midnight. He sat there through the jazz band playing mediocre renditions of songs by Miles, Trane, and Dizzy, but at least it wasn't that little dismal hotel room. He'd only had two drinks when they'd changed to the rock and roll band. There was a woman sitting at the bar. She was gorgeous, but Eddie wasn't looking for a woman. He didn't know what he was looking for that night, aside from wanting to feel alive again, to believe he knew who he was before he went home. On his way to the bathroom he'd accidentally knocked her jacket off the back of her chair. He'd apologized and made some stupid joke, which she laughed at, a laugh that rose from the core of the earth, filled with substance. It was all coming back to him as he held onto this strange woman and their kiss moved him from present to past and back again.

At the end of the night he'd walked her to the subway. She'd offered to see him again, but he told her the truth about being married and out of sorts. He was afraid he would fall apart as he said those words to her since he hadn't said anything to anyone about how he was feeling until that moment. Hell, he hadn't had much to say to anyone since he'd been back. He thought he might cry, and Eddie didn't cry in front of anyone. It was revealing too much to do a thing like that. But, before he could finish explaining, she'd leaned in and kissed him, and that kiss was the best kiss he'd ever had. It almost made him feel guilty since she wasn't Carleen. He didn't know if it was because of the timing or if it meant something about the two of them. All he knew was he felt the pieces of himself shift around inside and then reach out to connect him with another human being, deeply connect. When they finally came up for air, she laughed that laugh again, and somehow it was the cherry on top of the kiss.

"Don't look so surprised. I don't expect anything more and I'm not asking for anything from you. It's my gift to you. You went over there and fought for us, and it seems like you left some of you somewhere. I hope you find what you left over there so you can go home to your girl. I hope you find your happy again, Eddie."

Then she walked down the steps leaving him there feeling himself become alive again, instead of the empty reflection he'd seen that morning in the mirror. He found a pay phone and called Carleen and told her he was coming home.

Tangerines. Strawberries, and the ocean all over again.

When Eddie opened his eyes, she was gone.

He looked around the room. It was the same dismal, utilitarian room with ugly curtains and cheap furniture, but he felt different. He was still alive. Not the man he was before, but he didn't have to wait for death to come calling. Maybe there was something left in this world for him to hold onto. As he slowly dressed for the day, he decided he'd ask if he could have some fresh strawberries with his oatmeal this morning.

SCENTS AND ODORS & KISSING
What is memorable?
What do you like?
What do you hate?

Patchouli. I went to too many Grateful Dead concerts.
But, if a guy walked by and he looked like George Clooney and wearing good clothes!
I don't want to smell B.O.
The halitosis thing is a turn off.
Beer is okay, cigarettes—I don't mind it when I'm kissing; The last person I kissed who smoked, he also didn't smell like he smoked. (CAT)

I don't' like cigarette breath, but I have been okay with weed breath
Wine breath is different from liquor breath.

[What breath do you enjoy?]
Breath that has us in it and doesn't have other stuff in it.
Morning breath is odd. (DC)

Scents that you like:_____

HER PLACE

Something was new. She could feel it. She could feel herself being moved from one place, then into another, as if this place, her place, had changed. This was the place she'd been for a while and it felt like she belonged here. But something was different. Before there were times when she could stretch out parts of herself and it felt good. Right now, not so much. The space would get tight, then open up again, like it was before. It felt like she couldn't move. Because she didn't know time or units of time, she just waited until the squeezing stopped. She didn't know what "squeezing" meant, as a matter of fact; she just knew it would feel tighter, it would feel like she couldn't move and then stop.

All these new sensations started when the whole place changed. It went from being soft and like floating around, not that she knew what "floating" really meant. She just knew she liked the way it felt and then it was gone. What happened? Then the tightness started. Then it stopped. She was surprised and curious why it kept doing that thing. What is it? She wanted to ask those sounds she heard all the time. Why was it being repeated over and over?

"HUH-HUH-HUH!!"

"Keep going babe, you're doing great."

She thought about the other sounds she heard many times over and over again before today. "Hi Aja. Hi baby. Mommy loves you." What was a "mommy?" What was that about?

Sometimes she'd hear that sound and it was different. It was like a vibration, or something that made her place move in a nice way, but the sound wasn't the same--it was, "Aaaahhhhh," but it went up and down and felt like the way she'd move around. It felt like something pushing on her place, like a thump, thump, thump with other sounds around it. The Mommything was making a noise too. It was a good sound. "Hmmmm—hummmmmm." She was swinging in her place when that sound came. She could feel something warm outside her place and that thing was making the thump, thump, and the mommything was making that "Aaahhh" and "Hmmmm" sound . . . that's when she felt her top part get big and round. It made her feel funny inside, made her feel good.

Another squeeze happened and her place was changing again.

She was going somewhere!! Where was she going? Wherever it was she

didn't like it—it was squeezing her too much. For the first time ever, she

felt like she could make a sound like she was hearing, only she wanted to

make it really big. A BIG sound to make the squeezing stop. But she

couldn't... there was no way she could make a sound. She'd never made

a sound before. And her place was shifting to smaller and smaller. She

couldn't move anything. She felt like she was being squeezed all around.

Did the place hate her now? Did the place want her gone? Where would

she go? Why? She didn't want to go. She wanted to know if the

Mommything knew about this.

Then she heard new things. These things didn't sound warm and

her body didn't move to them and her top part didn't want to change

for that.

"PUSH!!"

"What is a push and why is my place getting smaller?" she asked

herself.

Then there was a sound that was different. This one scared her.

It sounded like the time that thing when The Mommy said, "Ginger is waiting to meet you," and that sound made her feel funny. Like a beating in the place, but it was faster and louder. Thump-thump, thump-thump

"I AM NEVER DOING THIS AGAIN! OH MY GOD!"

Then another sound… was this another Mommything? "I hear that a lot during this time, Terry. Just remember we're almost there."

"WE! THERE IS NO 'WE'! NOBODY IS RIPPING YOUR BODY IN HALF! IT'S FEELS LIKE I'M TRYING TO PUSH A CAR OUT OF ME! How much longer?!"

Was that The Mommything? Her sound was different. Maybe The Mommything was being squeezed tight, too. Why was this happening to both of them?

Then there was another sound and another all at once and over and over.

"Come on babe—"

"Aaauuugggggghhh! Shut up!"

"Terry breathe. Breathe and relax—"

"You relax! Put that damn camera down don't you dare take a picture of me like this!"

"You told me to capture everything. I'm trying to do what you wanted!"

"Do you think this is helping right now?"

"Okay, sorry. Sorry. Let's just focus on breathing—OH MY GOD! What is that?"

"We're almost there—"

"It's been twelve hours! Twelve hours—Fucking yoga didn't work at all!"

"Babe you know they said it COULD help—"

"What?! What are you saying?"

"Nothing. Sorry babe. Doctor, what should I do?"

"Okay, I'm sorry Ted. I'm sorry. It just hurts so much. Okay. We took the classes—we were both there, don't you remember what they said?" The Mommything sound was softer now.

"I don't remember—I'm sorry—I can't—CHRIST TERRY, I'M SORRY!" Now she recognized that sound too, that one sound came sometimes from the outside and it said things like "Can't wait to meet

you. I am your Daddy." What did that mean? "Meet you?"

"Just a few more. You can do this, Terry—"

"I don't really have a choice, do I?"

She heard all these sounds and she felt something she'd never

felt before, so many things. Her insides got all soft like the thing she was

in and then she felt like she wanted to go back to her place. But it was

tight—tight—tighter and then her top! Her top was stuck in something!

"The baby is crowning!"

"Is that her?! She's coming babe! You can do it!"

Her top was stuck, and she just wanted to go back to her place.

The place that she knew. If she could have she would have gone back to

her place.

"One more push, Terry!" from the sound that wasn't the

Mommything.

"Baby, I'm here. Here, squeeze my hand. Puuuuuusssshhhh—"

"Auugghhhhh!!!"

Then her eyes hurt, and it was too much of everything—because it had all changed and it was cold, and she felt all parts of herself moving and tingling and there wasn't anything squeezing her anymore. She felt like she was floating without the place around her and then something was in her and it made a loud sound she didn't like and then there was a new sound.

Wait, that sound was coming from her. What was going on? That sound was her? That was a BIG sound.

Then she was put on something warm, something soft and a little bit like her place, like she could slosh around in it. It wasn't as soft as her place, but it still felt like a good place to be. There was something new— something her top part noticed, like something warm and it felt weird, a little bad ... she felt things all over her. Then, she was floating around and suddenly, she could hear the same thing she heard when she was in her place. Thump- thump, thump-thump. But she wasn't right beside it. She was laying on it.

"Well, Terry, meet your daughter."

"She's beautiful."

"Oh babe, look at her, she's perfect."

It was The Mommy sound! And that one that is the Daddee … and who is that one there? Not the Ginger; it didn't sound like the Ginger anyway.

"Congratulations, Terry and Ted! What are you going to name her?"

The Mommy and The Daddee both made a sound, "Aja."

She felt herself wrapped up; it felt like being in her place. The Mommy kept doing something to her top. What is that? Whatever it was, it made her face big again.

"Look, she loves it when you kiss her, Terry. She's smiling! Oh my God, Terry, she's smiling already."

Then the Daddee did that thing and her top part got big again.

"She smiled for me too."

"I love her so much. Look what we did honey. I'm sorry Ted, about the yelling"

"After twelve hours of labor—I'm surprised you weren't throwing things."

"Yeah, me too. She's here. She's so beautiful. Hi Aja. Hello beautiful baby Aja."

And she laid there on The Mommy while she and The Daddy kept making sounds. Those sounds made her feel better than in her place. They kept doing that thing to her top part and it made her insides feel different. As she closed her eyes her face got big again every time they said, "Aja." She liked that sound. Aja. It was Aja and The Mommy and The Daddy in a new place for her.

Haiku #2

Your breath warm and sweet
A promise made without words
Lies, run for cover

WHAT WOULD YOU COMPROMISE ON WHEN IT COMES TO KISSING?

I don't know what I would compromise on if he's like a really, really bad kisser. Some people are trainable, like you could do stuff to let the person know you like things and they can change. Maybe if there was too much slobber I would compromise on that. (CAT)

Nothing
D.C.

FIRST KISS....

It was actually in the public library sometime in high school. I was 14-15, Freshman/sophomore
We were in the art section. It was some boy one of my friends had set me up to go out with. I didn't know him. He didn't go to our high school. My friend told me he works in the library. I don't know if we'd spoken on the phone. He said, "I want to show you something over here in the stacks." So I went with him over to the stacks. We were talking and he was flirting, and I lean in and that was it. I don't remember a lot about it except being there and liking it. I don't remember whether it was slurpy or not. (CAT)

Yes, her name was Faith.
What it was our parents use to play spades and bid whist and all the kids would be in a room (while they played). We ranged in age from eight to teenagers. Younger teenagers, maybe fourteen.
So spin the bottle happened and I really liked Faith, like she was my first crush. Fate just played a role in this. Like Cupid was sitting in the room. So like the bottle came around and one of the guys in the room I guess he noticed how I was looking at Faith cause when the bottle was spinning he manipulated it and

he caught it and it stopped on Faith. He said like, "You were spinning it too hard and I'm gonna stop it." So it stopped on Faith. Everybody was like, "Kiss her!" and she seemed a little embarrassed. I'd seen kisses on TV and in movies and everybody closed their eyes, so I closed my eyes. I think I kissed her nose. Everybody was like, "No, no do it again!" and Faith was so embarrassed that I opened my eyes and maybe I shouldn't have done that cause when I opened my eyes I saw the terrified look in her eyes. I tried – as much I was able to understand and feel empathy back then, but I was really digging the kiss too—you know like hey let's just do this and get it over with, but her eyes were just shifting all over the place and rolling back in her head. When we kissed this time I didn't close my eyes. I didn't even feel her lips cause now her eyes were more important. Like my first kiss—you know, I hit her nose and the second time was like to reassure her that everything was going to be okay. And then later Faith and I kind of looked at each other and we tried to do it right... so maybe that was my first kiss. Because then we really kissed, we both closed our eyes, we touched lips—I was ten. I will always remember that look in her eyes more than I than the feeling of the kiss. (DC)

I was infatuated with this boy. We actually had sex before we kissed. It was in college and it was the hardest I ever pursued anyone. When it finally came it was, Oh my God it was wonderful. It was very passionate. It was free. Oh my God. Not bearing down. It was just the lips, then a little bit of tongue. You know later in life it's all about the tongue, it's down your throat it's all over the place. ..... then the lips were actually numb. That's the scariest part. The lips got numb. It took place in a hotel room. We were on a project and had to drive back that day.

(Frank F)

HAIKU #3
Moonlight upon us
Lips, tongue, taste entwine sweetly
Rock heart will not break

Worst kiss EVER

Sometimes you know you can be out in a bar and you've had a few too many to drink and maybe smoking a little something you shouldn't have been smoking. Somebody decides to kiss you and they've got their tongue out. That happened once. At first I was like, "I'm not ready to kiss him." Then I started to back away. Don't suck on my tongue!! I think that's vile. I'm not for that. I also think that now that I'm an adult, you need to be able to kiss me without giving me a hickey. You should be able to kiss somebody on the neck and not leave a big ol' hickey on my neck. I don't need to walk around with that all day. (CR)

There've been so many. The double over the lip thing, too slobbery— oh and the teeth, when people bang their teeth against your teeth. It's like the opposite of too much tongue or like when they don't move their nose the right way so you clunk noses. The snake tongue—in and out, in and out! (CAT)

My worst kiss happened in like 2011 actually. I couldn't believe this woman did this. It was a date, a second date we didn't know each other that well, but we were attracted to each other. We went in for the kiss and she opened her mouth so wide I felt like she was trying to swallow my face. I was like, "What are you doing?" thinking in my head. I was trying to caress her face so I could like pull her mouth down a little bit and she wasn't getting it, so she opened her mouth even wider. I was like, "NO!" I have to tell you I got so tired of it, we went on about seven dates, I always hated that moment with her, and she was like pushing real hard like with her mouth, her face—everything was just pushed forward. Forced. So one day I said, we just really need to try to connect with our kisses. We would always kiss outside, they would be departure kisses, corner kisses. So, I thought maybe we should kiss inside. I said we should just try to connect through our kiss. I guess that statement must've really bothered her cause she texted me and said she didn't think we should see each other anymore. Maybe she caught what I was saying. It was too bad. But how do you teach an adult how to kiss or how to be with you in a kiss. (DC)

I remember an invasion of my mouth. They were on me and suddenly it felt like there was a boa constrictor cobra-tongue snaking its way [in my mouth] and I just wanted them out. OUT! That's all I could think of – Get out of my mouth. They didn't have to get away, but just get out of my mouth. That's really too rude. [Or] bite my chin. He bit me to the point that was I like if you draw blood motherfucker... He was like all over my face. He was like on me and then he was nibbling my nose, and then slid his tongue over here and then all of a sudden he just went: CHOMP!!! I felt like a German Shepard just took my chin in his mouth. I thought "You lost points. Okay? You lost points—because it wasn't so bad up to there."

It's all about pressure to me. The right amount of pressure. It's like anything with touching somebody. I felt like he was trying to prove, like THIS IS HOT and he was dominant, and I was like get my chin out of your mouth and take your teeth off my chin. It was like Hannibal! Okay, Hannibal, get some fava beans go to it, but not on my chin. Too much aggression.

Too little intensity feels—you need to feel the need, the want to kiss. I feel like that's where the hand behind the head, pressure on the lips comes from and if you overdo it then somebody's grinding my face into a cinderblock. If it's intense, you kind of feel like you do want to be a part of each other. There's a softness there. There's an intensity, there's a certain amount of lip on lips pressure.

[ALSO] Too anything. Too bossy. Like "come over here!" I'm like what are you, Stanley Kowalski? Or an inopportune moment. Someone's like "I'd really like to kiss you." Like you're at the bar and you've met them – like five minutes ago. ... and they want to kiss you and I'm like, "I'm not sure I want to.." (VB)

COOL ENOUGH

"Bryan! Bryan!"

He knew it was Ali, short for Alicia, his best friend. He'd been trying to escape before she caught up with him. Bryan didn't want to disappoint her about the dance this Saturday, but he was going to have to do it. He couldn't think of any other way to save himself the embarrassment he was sure to happen.

"DUDE! Slow down!" Ali caught up with him and draped her arm around his shoulders.

Ali was fifteen, some days she acted like she was going on six and others, thirty. She was worldly, wise, and absolutely spoiled. She had dark curly hair, bronze skin, and gray eyes. He could've been in love with her, but he wasn't, something they'd recently confirmed.

"Hey Ali, what's up?"

"We gotta talk about Saturday. This is going to be lit son!"

"Lit? Really? Son? Who are you trying to sound like now?" he chuckled.

"Jameel was teasing me the other day. Said I talked like a white girl."

"You are a white girl—"

She playfully shoved him, "Only half. Don't try distracting me. When do you want to get together to practice our routine? I found a GREAT SONG! I can't wait, it is going to be lit—fantastic!"

"I don't know, Ali. I really don't feel like--"

"Aw c'mon! Just like for a half hour and we'll nail it, son—wait! Are you saying? Oh, no, no—you can't just back out--" It was the beginning of an 'Ali Tantrum.' When he didn't respond, she dropped her backpack on the sidewalk. "Seriously?! That's all we've been talking about for the past few weeks! Why?"

All this drama was the last thing he wanted to deal with today. Especially today.

"I need to finish the essay for Stinky-Stewart, this weekend," he said using the nickname for their English teacher, Mr. Stewart, who always smelled like day old tuna fish. "I was supposed to have it done by today and I didn't, so I have to focus on that over the weekend. Not some stupid dance."

"Stupid dance?!! IT'S OUR JUNIOR PROM BRY!!"

He hated it when she spoke in exclamations. Honestly, he really didn't have much to do on the essay for Mr. Stewart's class save a concluding paragraph, but she didn't know that, and she didn't need to know it.

"Yeah, well, this essay makes or breaks me dude. I'm like right on the cusp of a--"

"An A. You're always on the cusp of an A, and you always get the A, so stop freaking out. What's really going on? You were all excited about it two weeks ago--this whole thing was partly your idea."

She was right and she knew something was wrong. He and Ali had been best friends since third grade when he'd kicked a kid for shoving her down and calling her the 'n' word. He was taller than her back then a lot taller; now they were both about the same height. He was lean and lanky; she was full of curves already. Where Bryan was shy, Alicia was loud and boisterous, and she knew she was beautiful, which only frustrated her in this school where she was treated like a pariah. They both were since they'd been in the gifted classes and skipped two grades, so they were the youngest kids in eleventh grade. In other ways though Alicia was born to get her way. He wasn't. Bryan was afraid of many things, things he didn't understand, the kind of things that clung to the edges of his understandings.

"What? Are you just going to stand there and ignore me? Why did you change your mind?"

"It was a stupid idea from the beginning, okay?" He started walking away. "I was thinking about it last night and realized it's just dumb."

"No, it's not! Besides, I was looking forward to it. What's the big deal?"

Feeling backed into a corner he decided to end this conversation right now. "I told you I have things to do—"

"Just out of nowhere? Really? Sounds like bullshit to me—"

"I JUST DON'T WANT TO GO, OKAY?! Give a rest Ali." And he walked away from her. He didn't have tantrums, but when he put his foot down, that was that. Ali and everyone in his family knew he had a stubborn streak that was like concrete. Immovable.

It was easier this way, be stubborn, alleviate opportunities for discussion. Cut all conversation about it off because he couldn't explain to her that he'd changed his mind due to who was going to be there. He couldn't tell her that because then she'd want to know what difference that would make, which would open a can of worms he wasn't ready to deal with in this moment.

Right now, he just felt bad. He stopped and looked back at her. "Ali this grade is more important to me than some dance. Okay? Why can't you understand that?" She pouted; he couldn't believe she still pouted at fifteen. What a frigging baby, but she was pretty much his only friend. He walked back to her, dropped his backpack, and hugged her.

They stood that way for a minute in silence and comfort, then Ali leaned back and stared into his blue eyes. She brushed the thick wave of brown hair out of his eyes that often fell forward hiding the cloud of freckles on his cheeks and nose.

She sighed, "Okay, alright. I get it—actually, no, I don't, but I know I can't make you do something you don't wanna."

They picked up their respective backpacks and walked in silence for a few minutes. She bumped into him with her shoulder and he laughed. He could never stay mad at Ali. Not just because he wouldn't have anyone to talk to or hang out with if he did, but because she was Ali The Magnificent. At least to him she seemed magnificent, beautiful, and the coolest person he'd ever met, and he wished he could be in love with her.

"So what should we binge on Saturday night? I've already caught up on *Stranger Things*."

"I do have to get this essay done, but maybe later. Your place or mine?"

"Let's do mine. My parents are going out to a dinner with friends. How much of the essay do you really have to get done?"

"I can finish by seven, I think."

"Seven! We could still—never mind. Okay, we'll order in and--"

"My treat—"

"Damn right. I was really looking forward to dancing all night with you-"

"Ali."

"I give, I give, okay? But, I'm just sayin', you know?"

"We can dance at your place—"

"Yeah, but the being all dressed up part and seeing the faces of all the asshats who pick on us every chance they get—just imagine their faces when they'd see us dressed up and doing our routine—and we worked so hard on that routine Bry. I just found the BEST SONG-- Okay, sorry, dropped. Done."

"I'm sorry Ali, but you know we'll have a better time with just the two of us. Who do we have to prove anything to—"

"It wasn't about proving anything to anyone…. it's just that."
She was silent.

Bryan was afraid to look at her because he didn't want to see her crying. He could never handle seeing Ali in tears. He'd never had been able to stand it. He bumped into her to make her laugh, but she moved away.

"What?" And when she didn't respond, "Ali? What is it?"

"Nothing." After a minute or two she stopped walking and

plopped down on the curb. A habit she had of sitting anywhere at all that he considered gross, but he joined her, while thinking he'd have to put these jeans in the laundry sooner than he'd expected. He'd hoped to wear them at least twice more. Not happening after this, oh well.

Ali stared off into space for a moment and he waited patiently. Actually, he was thinking about the relief he felt knowing that he could avoid the possibility of feeling like crap all through the dance on Saturday and possibly the rest of the school year.

"It's just that" Ali twisted her mouth into a pucker while she put the words together, "It isn't that I want to prove anything to those jerks. I just wanted to feel like I could go have a good time just like they do. I can be pretty—"

"What are you talking about? You are pretty Ali—"

"You're my best friend. You have to say shit like that—"

"No, I don't. Ali, you're gorgeous and you know it—"

"Then why didn't anyone ask me to be their date? Why doesn't anyone ever ask me to be their date? Or why don't any of the guys around here ask me hang out with them? I love hanging out with you

Bry, but sometimes I want some guy to like me, like, LIKE me, you know?" She was silent as she fished around in her backpack. She pulled out her sunglasses and put them on, while she answered her own question. "Naw, I get it. It's one of the many joys of being one of the only six black kids at this school—and the black kids don't like me cause I'm not really black and because we were skipped and I can't help it if I'm smart and-- God, I hate this school."

Bryan thought the sunglasses meant hiding, which means she's about to cry. Damn.

"They don't like us because they don't get our kind of cool Ali, that's all. We have our own special kind of cool."

"Right, sure, and that's why Courtney Wilson called me all kinds of names yesterday after class, her and those bitches in her little group always go in on me. She said me that I sucked up to Ms. Howard so I could get the A in World History—"

"And what grade did Courtney get? I saw the grades posted— she got a C, just barely. They're haters. That's all."

"You don't get it."

"Yes, I do—"

"No, you don't because you are the coolest of the cool. You don't give a shit about what anybody thinks. You don't care. If you asked any girl out they'd say yes—"

"I'm not interested in anyone at that school. They're all so plastic and—and phony—and I have to stay focused on my grades. Prioritization, Ali, okay? I like being in the gifted classes. I've got plans after we get out of here and they don't include having my GPA drop. Last year I almost failed algebra and environmental science both."

"That's why you don't get it. You don't… don't need that kind of thing. Being you, being white, has perks—Okay?" She shook her head in frustration and emitted a growl deep in her throat, "Auggghh. I can't explain it to you—okay, like I would love it if just once one of the guys asked me out or to hang out for lunch or even talked to me. They just tease me—and I hate it. And, I know they think I'm cute. I can tell!"

A single tear rolled down her cheek, evading the sunglasses. He wiped it away and put his arm around her.

"You know I think you're amazing, right?" He whispered into her hair.

"Stop." And she playfully pushed him away. "I couldn't like you like that. We've gone through that already, remember? You're my Boy Bry-Bry"

"I hate when you call me Bry-Bry"

"Yeah, but that's what you are to me." She stood up and tousled his hair, which Bryan also hated, then took off running, "Last one to the store is buying Skittles—the big bag!"

They ran, him behind her. Him shortly catching up to her, and then passing her as they reached the entrance to the corner store.

"Ha! I win! That'll be a bag of chips please," he said laughing.

"Skittles—"

"Nope I want chips today."

They entered the store together, the two, too cool but not cool enough kids wanting to belong. That's how Bryan thought of them and he was okay with that for now.

On his way to Ali's house on Saturday he stopped to pick up snacks for the night. His essay and chores around the house done, he felt relieved about everything. Bryan was also glad to escape his parent's prying questions and the concerned looks they gave him earlier in the day.

"Your mom and I thought you were going to the dance tonight with Ali what happened?" his father had asked when he found Bryan lounging around the kitchen eating cereal for a snack a few hours ago. "Shouldn't you be getting ready?"

"We changed our minds. We're going to hang out over Ali's and watch some movies."

"Oh, but I washed that nice blue button-down shirt especially for you tonight, and I was going to let you borrow that silver and black tie you like," his dad said.

"Thanks, but, we have more fun hanging out just the two of us, so we decided not to go."

His mom came into the room, "Did I hear you say you're not going to the prom? Did you and Ali have a fight?"

"No Mom. We just decided we'd rather chill without all the jerks hanging around—"

His mother put down the pan of lasagna she was making. Her voice turning serious, "Are they still picking on you? Because if they are—"

"No Mom. We'd just rather hang out by ourselves. I'll be home by eleven."

He'd scooted out of the kitchen before they could dig in deeper with the whys and why nots and all the other questions. Once his dad had even insinuated that he thought he and Ali were more than friends and tried to suggest that they were both really young, but he knew kids these days were more "active" than he thought they should be, and he wanted to encourage him to "be careful." Ewwww. Gross.

As he was ringing Ali's doorbell arms loaded with goodies, he was looking forward to a night of being chill and safe, maybe a little dancing, and they could watch the entire new season of American Horror Story. Ali opened the door, grinning.

"Hey. S'up."

"Hey, S'up."

Ali repeated, "S'up choo?"

Bryan made his voice deep, "S'up choo?" He walked into the foyer as they both laughed at their private joke of mimicking the jocks at school.

"What's the joke?" Bryan heard a familiar voice and his stomach tightened.

"What the hell?" he thought.

"Hey Quentin, it's—it's" he stammered. This was totally unexpected and unwelcome.

Ali stared at him for a brief moment. He could tell she knew something was wrong, "It's just this thing we do—we're not trying to be cool like that, to do it for real and anyway, it's just a stupid, private joke. Quentin you know Bryan right?"

"Yeah, we had algebra together for minute last year. How you doin', man?"

"I'm good." Bryan quickly moved into the kitchen. "I picked up some snacks—I thought it was just, you know, Ali, so I got stuff for two people—we can share though."

Looking through the bag, Ali said, "Dude! What are you talking about? There's enough snacks here for the entire eleventh grade. You okay Bry?"

"Yeah, sure. Gotta use your bathroom though."

"You know where it is. I'll put the sodas in the fridge and bring the rest of the stuff in the living room. You can meet us in there. We're going to watch *Black Mirror* first." She pulled out a giant bag of Skittles, "DAMN DUDE! You must feel real guilty about canceling our plans you've got all my favs here!"

"Plans?" Quentin asked, looking at Bryan.

"Yeah, we were—we had this stupid idea"

Ali cut him off. "We planned on going to the dance tonight, had our own dance routine worked out and everything, but Bry had an English paper to finish, so here we are."

"Wow, aren't you the good student? Outstanding!"

Bryan wasn't sure if he was being sarcastic or if he meant what he was saying, which flustered him even more. "Why aren't you at the dance?" Bryan was trying his best not to show his nervousness, but his stomach was flipping back and forth, and he was certain he was trembling.

"I have no interest in dances. It's all a bunch of bull man."

"I ran into Quentin while I was out riding my bike. He and I got to talking, and he was saying it was all bullshit—same as you and me feel about it—the school and everything! So I figured he could hang out with us tonight. You don't mind, do you?"

Like he had any choice, "Naw, no worries. Be back in a minute."

Bryan went into the bathroom closed the door and leaned against it. He closed his eyes. This was totally messed up! The person he had wanted to avoid at the dance was here. He didn't want to see Quentin Walcottt dancing with some girl like Erica Dayton, or whomever his flavor of the month was right now. Or worse, for someone else to see him staring at Quentin with puppy dog eyes. He flashbacked to last year's algebra class when the two of them had sat next to each other. It started off as cool, lots of fun because they had so much in common. Then things got scary for him. *"What was that?"* he'd find himself thinking when some errant thought caught him off guard like the time Quentin threw his arm around his shoulder and he had fought the urge to lay his head on his shoulder. If the kids were mean to him before because of his grades, what would happen if he had done that and someone saw. Or what if the unthinkable happened and Quentin got pissed at him?

Shortly thereafter he'd find his mind wandering and distracted in algebra. Suddenly, parenthetical equations that he'd normally complete in his sleep became too complicated. They demanded too much attention during class while his mind was on Quentin. Fixated on Quentin. Quentin with his blonde curly hair, dimples, and brilliant, lopsided smile. Quentin who was tall and not lean but built like the football player he used to be in tenth grade. He continued to tell himself this preoccupation with Quentin was a phase that he would soon pass through. Like the moon going through different phases. Soon, he would be a full moon again, no missing pieces hiding in the shadows, thinking about Quentin.

One day he had the bright idea to try to change his seat in class. Bryan had come into the room early enough for Mr. Bennett to notice and mention it to him. Some dry dad joke that Bryan obligatorily laughed at as he sat in the only empty seat in the room since Cynthia Grant had moved away. It was the perfect inconspicuous spot since it was back in the corner near the cabinets. Bryan had slumped down in the seat in the hopes of not drawing anyone's attention, especially Quentin's, that he wasn't in his regular seat.

Instead Quentin walked into the room and spotted him immediately. He did the crooked half smile that made Bryan's heart flutter and then strolled back towards him. All he said was "Cool. I get it dude." Bryan was too afraid to say anything, so he'd just nodded. Then Quentin asked Michael Harris to change seats with him, which Michael did. Dammit. Throughout the rest of the class period Quentin had slouched down in his seat, like Bryan was doing, and every now and then he would paste that smile on his face and look at Bryan. Bryan felt obligated to smile back. Why? He had no idea, but he couldn't stop himself if he wanted to. The same way he couldn't stop the roller-coaster from flying around in his stomach every time Quentin looked at him or touched him.

At the end of the period Quentin put his hand out for a fist bump,

"That's right, dude, don't do what they expect. We gotta change things without their permission. It's our world now."

Bryan's mind was racing so much that he had no idea what he was talking about, but he fist-bumped him back, "Later dude." As he walked towards his next class, he told himself he was screwed. He had no idea what he needed to do to fix this.

He began feigning sickness to get out of class. He'd finally asked to switch to another algebra class, but by then it was too late-- he was failing. On top of that he had to make up some excuse to explain to Quentin why he wasn't in that class anymore. It was lame. Something about having problems with another teacher and how he'd gone to the principal and asked for help. So, they changed his schedule all around in order to put him in the different class. He'd had to make up a different story to tell the principal about being sleepy that early in the morning, and could he *please* change to a different class because he really wanted to do well in algebra.

It was during the beginning of the spring semester when everything went way left for Bryan. On the first day of the new semester he saw Quentin sitting in the second row of their environmental science class. They'd waved at each other, but he seemed preoccupied. It didn't take long to figure out what was going on. Erica Dayton came in and Quentin moved the book from the desk next to him that he'd apparently put there to hold the seat for her. Bryan was sitting in the next to the last row, attempting to be as low-key as possible, but it was clear that he could've been laying on the floor choking to death and Quentin wouldn't give a damn. He was all eyes and smiles for Erica. When the bell rang for the end of the period, he realized he hadn't heard a thing the teacher had said. He waited a few minutes, then followed Quentin and Erica just to see if his suspicions were correct. That's all-- he just wanted to see.

He saw. He saw Quentin slip his arm around Erica's shoulders and she cuddled in his arms. He wondered how she could do that while they were walking. Then he saw Quentin's hand brush her butt and she giggled. Bryan felt his whole chest cave in. He felt like he couldn't breathe. He wasn't sure why he was freaking out. He wasn't sure why he couldn't concentrate whenever Quentin was around. He wasn't sure why he thought about Quentin as he was trying to fall asleep at night and looked for him everywhere he went. He didn't have many friends; he was a loner. It was just he and Ali. He began to imagine what it would be like to be Bryan, Quentin, and Ali. Or, maybe sometimes it could just be Quentin and Bryan. He wasn't positive about what was going on, but he had a good idea and again he convinced himself it was only a phase. Bryan had read about those kinds of things happening at a certain age. He'd google it when he got home. What he needed to search he wasn't sure, but he had an idea.

He peered around the hallway corner just in time to see Erica leaning against her locker and Quentin leaning into her. The muscles of his biceps were still visible through the thin, blue cotton shirt he wore as they contracted when he put his weight on his arms to encircle her. His wavy blonde hair was just long enough to create shadows on her face as he leaned into her. Bryan imagined what it would be like to look into his hazel eyes like Erica was doing right now. Her foot jiggled and she giggled again. Just then Quentin gently caressed her face as he leaned forward towards her. Bryan wondered what it would feel like for Quentin to caress him like that. Quentin was moving closer and closer to her. He was going to kiss her!!

He moved quickly in the opposite direction down the stairs towards the parking lot while questioning himself. "What is wrong with you? What are you some kind of freakin' stalker? Dude! So what if he kisses her? So what? He's a dude. You're a dude. So. Fucking. What?"

He was halfway out the door when he realized he hadn't written down his homework from his last class. As he went up the stairs back to the classroom Ali was coming down. In a panic, he reached out and grabbed her hand, something he had never done before.

"Bry! What's wrong?"

"Nothing. I forgot to write down my environmental science homework. Walk with me?'

"Okay." He saw her quickly look down at their two hands joined as if it were some kind of alien baby or something. "You okay?"

"Yeah. Just missed you today, that's all. I haven't seen you at all."

"What? DUDE! We ate lunch together."

"Well, I don't feel like we really had a chance to talk, you know?" He said still holding her hand. Ali being Ali started swinging her arm while they walked, which caused them to break out in giggles. His panic began to subside.

"I just need to take a picture of the board with the homework assignment."

Fortunately, Ms. Clawson, the teacher, wasn't in the room—he didn't want to have to explain why he hadn't copied or photographed the board during class. The door was open, so he and Ali quietly slipped in. She was standing right behind him. He took the picture and as he turned, he looked into her eyes, and with a question materializing in his head, he kissed her. At first it was a quick peck.

"Okay. Whatever, dude," she said and pecked him on the cheek too.

Then Bryan really kissed her. It was his first real kiss with tongue and everything. He had seen some of the senior guys kissing girls before, so he copied their moves. He put his hand behind her head, he nibbled on her lip, he slipped his tongue into her mouth. Ali pushed away from him.

"BRYAN! You gave me tongue! DUDE!!!"

Ms. Clawson stepped into the room, "Bryan? Alicia? What's going on?"

"I just—I left my notebook, so I came back." He could feel his face turn crimson all over. He charged out of the room, leaving Ali and Ms. Clawson staring after him.

It wasn't long before he heard Ali calling after him.

"Bryan!"

But he just kept walking as fast as he could and left her behind. He didn't know how to explain himself to her. He couldn't explain it to himself and he just couldn't deal with any questions from anyone right now. He practically ran home. By the time he'd reached the corner he no longer heard Ali calling him, and for that he was glad. He decided it would be best to give her space for a few days.

On the following Friday, the first Friday of the new semester, Ali cornered him at his locker. "Don't say shit."

She grabbed his arm and walked him towards the back exit of the school. He didn't fight. She was going to yell at him; he knew he had it coming. He'd just take his medicine in silence. In truth, he'd been terrified that he'd ruined his only friendship, the best friendship he imagined he'd ever have in his life. Bryan had been trying to figure out a way to approach her to try to explain everything to her. He wasn't ready for it, couldn't figure it out, not how to explain it at least, not at all. Instead, he'd let it ride. He'd considered going over to her house and trying to talk to her but then he wasn't sure she'd even talk to him. When she grabbed his arm, he was actually relieved because at least she was going to talk to him. If she yelled, he'd apologize and claim heat stroke or too much sugar or something – anything and hope she'd forgive him.

When the door closed Ali pushed him against the wall and pressed against him while kissing him full on, with tongue and everything. Then she stepped back and stared at him.

"Okay, so we're even?"

He stammered, "I-I-I guess—I mean"

"Look Bry…" She pulled a Twizzler out of her pocket and chewed on it. This was her nervous tic, when she was worked up Ali gnawed on Twizzlers, they were her candy habit. "You are my BOY. You mean the world to me. But when we kiss—don't take this the wrong way--there's nothing there, and when I kiss the right guy, or girl, for that matter, I imagine I will feel something."

"Ali I—"

"I don't mean that I expect the world to shake or angels to sing, all like 'Aaaaahhh' or nothing like that—but DUDE, something's gotta move, and you just don't move me like that. I love you Bry, but not like that. Okay?" Ali began to walk towards the front of the school since the back door locked from the inside and Bryan followed her wanting to get past the mess he'd made of their friendship.

"Yeah. Sure."

"So, let's not do that EVER again. Cool?"

"Yeah. "

"Don't mean to break your heart or nothin'—did I break your heart?"

"No—I mean, well... I wasn't sure.... like I was wondering about us," he lied, because it all he could think to justify all of it. "You know, after all these years—and you know?"

"Oh, yeah, I get it, Bry, we spend so much time together my mom and dad actually kind of thought that maybe that was a thing with us too, but it's like I told them 'eeeew—'"

"Eeewww?"

"I don't mean, like you're ewww, but like, you're MY BOY. We can't roll like that. You're like my BLOOD DUDE!! Ya feel me?"

Ali was imitating her older brother Jameel again, even down to his swagger. Still, this was much better than Bryan trying to explain everything to her, which he couldn't if he wanted to, so he said, "Yeah. I feel ya."

"Bet. Now let's get to lunch and talk about that idea of yours and our plans for the dance."

The dance. That damn dance was coming up and he didn't want to go, but after the kissing debacle he couldn't get weird with this too. This had all happened a few days before he'd told Ali he didn't want to go to the dance. Now, Bryan had finally figured out the best way to handle it if Quentin was there with Erica, or any other girl, was for him not to be there. To avoid Quentin at all costs. Yet, here he was in the living room, hanging out with them instead of dancing. This could be bad was all that Bryan could think of and he couldn't just leave. Not after the kiss and he'd blown off the dance with Ali. She would not forgive him for it, or let it rest if he bailed on this as well. He told himself it was time for him to put his big boy pants on and act like he had some self-control. He could do that, couldn't he? He asked his image in the mirror over the bathroom sink.

"You can do this, right? Yes, I can. I can. I can. I can," he told his reflection.

There was a knock on the door, "Hey Bry? You okay? What are you doing?"

He splashed water on his face and flushed the toilet. His voiced cracked like it used to back when he was twelve and going through puberty, "What do you think I'm doin'?!" He cleared his throat. "I'll be out in a minute," Bryan said in a practiced, calmer tone of voice.

When he emerged from the bathroom Ali looked at him with concern, her light brown brows knitting together, "What's going on with you?"

"Nothing."

"Yeah, right. Tell that to someone who doesn't know you." She blocked his path down the hallway towards the kitchen with her body. "You have been so weird lately, what's up with you? Don't make me go all in on you, which I will, even though you are my BOY."

Bryan was confused, and a little disoriented. Quentin Walcott, one of the coolest, most desired boys in eleventh grade was in the living room when he was supposed to be at a dance, slobbering all over Erica or some other lusty girl, and Bryan was supposed to be safely ensconced with his best friend Ali. Safe. He was supposed to be safe. He considered begging off and lying to Ali to escape. He could say his stomach was messed up. No, no, he couldn't; he'd had this argument with himself already in the bathroom.

"So? You gonna answer?"

"What? I'm fine. I ran over here carrying those bags and I think I overdid it, that's all."

"Really? What are you some fragile damsel from one of those novels we're reading in English? What the hell is going on with you

DUDE?!"

"Stop yelling," he whispered furiously to her.

He was moving towards the living room to take a peek in and see what Quentin was doing. Actually, he just wanted to buy some time to come up with a better lie.

"Are you—are you like, like, I don't know, trying to get with Quentin?" he asked her.

Bryan didn't think so, but if she was, that made this situation even worse than it already was for him.

"WHAT?! "

"Ali? Please stop yelling I—"

Quentin was suddenly there in the hallway. "Hey, everything okay?"

Both of them stammered, Ali surprised by Bryan's question, and Bryan caught off guard by Quentin's nearness.

"Uhh, no—what? Yeah, we're good," Ali spluttered.

"Yeah—we're cool—just talking about, talking about something coming up."

Quentin took one look at both of their red faces, "Okay, Maybe I should go. I didn't mean to be like a third wheel or nothing"

Both Ali and Bryan said, "What?! Eeewww!" at the same time.

"DUDE! You've gotta be kidding me—it's nothing like—" Ali looked horrified.

"No, nothing like that—we're good," Bryan said walking away. The hallway was tight quarters. Quentin's proximity was too much for him.

Bryan went into the kitchen got a soda and opened it and then opened a can of Pringles, Ali's favorite, while he listened to their conversation. He didn't have a choice since Ali was being very loud as she explained that they had considered having a relationship but come to the mutual conclusion that the most they could be was best friends and that was enough for both of them. He could hear Quentin's laughter as she discussed in detail how they'd tried kissing and they both thought it was awful. Bryan downed almost a half of a stack of Pringles in one ferocious mouthful, almost choking and chased it with a long swallow of soda.

He heard Ali say, "So, you see there's nothing there. Bry-Bry is my BOY! That's all."

Quentin laughed, "Bry-Bry? Wow."

In went another mouthful of Pringles and he finished off the soda and was looking at the chocolate bar as his next conquest. Maybe, he thought, if I stuff my face I'll get sick for real and then I can leave here. It couldn't happen soon enough for him. Just as Quentin and Ali came around the corner Bryan released a giant burp.

"Bwwwwwaaaaaaaap!!" He turned absolutely crimson, looking into Quentin's eyes.

There was a moment of silence. Then Quentin and Ali began to laugh. Relieved, Bryan joined in.

"DUDE!! That was awesome!" Ali clapped, "Let me try, "she chugged down half a liter bottle of soda and burped.

Both Bryan and Quentin laughed.

Bryan stole a look at Quentin. He was surprised to find that he was looking at him and they both smiled.

"My turn." Quentin said and he popped open a liter of soda and started to drink it.

"Wait," Bryan said, "You've gotta help it along with eating something. Here." He handed him the open can of Pringles. Their fingers touched and he wondered if he'd imagined the spark he felt and the fleeting smile on Quentin's face. He told himself that he was being hopeful and that was the end of it.

The night went much better than Bryan had hoped. He gave space to Ali and Quentin just in case that was the way things were meant to go. He'd leave them in the living room alone and take extra time in the kitchen while he was replenishing their snacks. Or, when they put on music to dance, he stayed on the other side of the room so they could dance together. Ali and Bryan even taught Quentin their routine and repeated it over and over until they all collapsed in a heap on the floor. They laid there tangled up, sweaty, and over saturated with sugar.

"I need some water," Bryan said, and he went into the kitchen.

He caught sight of himself in the window over the kitchen sink. He looked at himself and smiled. Inside though, he knew he wasn't exactly happy. If Quentin and Ali ended up being together, then that had to be okay. She was his best friend. He was her BOY. Eventually he'd figure out how to deal with them being together. He understood and accepted what was what. He looked into his eyes, and told himself, "This is what it is. This is who I am and he's not mine to have. No more denial. You just can't." All kinds of questions were banging around in his head-- who to tell? Could he tell Ali? Would his parents be cool? What would he do if anyone in school decided this was another reason to bully him? He knew they would, because that's what they did. He'd seen it with another kid in the school. Could he handle it if they found out? Who would he date? Too many questions.

"Hello? Earth to Bry-Bry. DUDE!!" Ali was standing next to him.

"What? Quit yelling at me."

"I've been trying to get your attention for like the past five minutes. You okay?" She leaned against the cabinet.

"Just thinking. That's all."

"No shit. Off in another dimension."

She dropped her voice, "Seriously, you've been weird all night. I'm worried about you."

"No worries, DUDE. I'm good."

"Hey Bry, what are you gonna do?" she whispered.

"About what?"

"What? Duh" she looked behind her. "Look Q's in there—"

It took him a minute to realize that she'd given Quentin his own

nickname. She just stared at him while he tried to figure out what she

meant.

"He's not my type," she whispered, even more conspiratorially.

"We made out for a minute. Nothing. Zip. Dude, I think I'm never gonna

find someone who moves me, you know?" Ali, brushed her hair back and

her eyes glistened with moisture that she refused to let fall. "I think, I

think it was a pity kiss. God, I hate that."

They'd kissed while he was in the kitchen figuring out his shit. He

didn't know if he should be happy that she wasn't moved, sad for his

friend, or for both of them because Quentin was not for either of them.

He pulled Ali to him and held her close. He could hear her sniffle, then

clear her throat.

She whispered into his shoulder, "This was supposed to be a fun night Bry. I'm sorry."

"Hey, everything okay?" Quentin was standing in the kitchen doorway.

Ali, turned her head, wiping her tears surreptitiously, so he couldn't see and without looking at Quentin, but at Bryan meaningfully, "I need to go upstairs for minute. I forgot to call my mom and dad, let them know we haven't burned the house down." She quickly left the kitchen and went up the stairs avoiding Quentin as she did.

Quentin moved next to Bryan. "She alright? Did I do something wrong?"

"Naw, she'll be back down. She always calls her parents when we're here for a while," he lied. "Want some more soda?"

"I think I need to drink some water. We really pounded that junk food," Quentin said, looking at the table littered with wrappers, bags, and empty soda bottles. "I probably won't sleep for two days. I never eat this much sugar."

"Wish I could say that."

The silence that followed was awkward and long.

"I may have… I think I screwed up," Quentin said, turning around so he faced the kitchen window.

Bryan didn't know what to say, so he shrugged and started to clear up the mess on the table.

Quentin sighed, "So, she's your best friend, right? I mean, I see you guys together all the time. I thought for a minute you two were, you know like, together—I know you're not, now."

Bryan didn't want to have this conversation. He was still knotted up about everything and he didn't like that Ali was upstairs possibly crying. He started thinking he should go up and see about her. How was he supposed to handle all of this emotional crap? This was not his comfort zone. His feelings for Quentin, his best friend being a mess, and the possibility that maybe Quentin and Ali could be together. It was one kiss for crap sake. Maybe he should send Quentin upstairs to see about Ali and they could … he couldn't bring himself to picture it. His insides were a roiling mess and it wasn't from all the junk food.

"I don't know what you want me say. You know, why don't you—I mean-- did you like kissing her?"

Quentin turned red and turned to stare at Bryan. "Wow. I mean, like she told you huh?"

Sarcastically Bryan responded, "We ARE best friends. Why are you here Quentin? You could've been at the dance tonight—I know you said you don't like those kinds of things, but I don't believe you." Suddenly, Bryan felt he needed to protect Ali. "You could've been there with any of the "cool girls" who swoon over you all the time. Instead you're here playing with Ali's feelings. That is so not right dude."

Quentin looked cowed, "I'm sorry, I just…"

"You just what? Don't you dare go back and make jokes about us, okay? I may not be able to kick your ass, but I'll find someone and do their homework for a whole year who will do it for me if I hear one person tell a joke about you and Ali. She's a good person-- and she was trying to be nice to you and--"

Bryan didn't see it coming. He was totally surprised. Quentin had moved next to him, taken his face in his hands, and began to kiss him.

There were no words for everything rushing through his body in this moment. It was beyond time standing still. It was beyond whatever he would've imagined if he could've imagined. It was if a lock had been turned and each chamber fell into place for a release and a connection at the same time. He had no idea how long they kissed. Once they stopped for air, he leaned his forehead against Quentin's and then he sought out his mouth again. Quentin responded, hungrily kissing and holding him.

When they finally came up for air.

"I didn't know." Bryan said.

"I wasn't sure. That's why I came here tonight. I wanted to know."

"Why did you make out with Ali? She's going to be hurt."

"I thought she wanted it and I wasn't sure—sometimes I try to you know? Like … I try to date girls and—and… it just never works. It's not for me. I wondered about us—I mean I thought that … anyway…. but then last year you transferred out of algebra, so I figured I had it all wrong and…" His voice faltered.

They looked deeply into each other's eyes for a moment. Bryan leaned into him, they hugged and kissed again. This time was better than the first for Bryan.

"You weren't wrong. I was …. I was kinda scared? I guess," he whispered into Quentin's ear.

Bryan felt such intensity and he didn't know exactly what to do with all of these feelings, but he knew he needed to take a step back. He did.

"I'm sorry, I don't know what this means."

"It means, that we like each other. That I want to spend time with you. That, I hope, you want to spend time with me—"

"I've never done anything like—"

"Yeah, me neither. Never done anything with anyone—nothing serious. I think the best thing is…. we can take it slow; you know. No worries, no pressure."

Bryan ran his hand through his hair. "Yeah. Okay." He figured he would go home and Google what he should do, how this should work, because this was all new to him. "We have to tell Ali, though. I can't lie to her."

He figured it was better to do it now and get it over with. After all, it didn't seem like she was into Quentin, but he could be wrong. He slowly climbed the stairs trying to figure out how to broach the subject, how to tell her. He knocked softly on her bedroom door.

"Entre´!" She was sitting on her bed watching a movie on her tablet.

"Hey, you okay?"

"How are YOU?" she smiled at him. "You guys didn't come up for air for a long time. Geez, I thought you might be going to do something really kind of nasty in the kitchen. Eeewww!"

Bryan, stuttered, "You—you saw?"

"Heck yeah. Seriously, Bry-Bry, I'm good. Q and I have no chemistry, not like you two, that was positively explosive DUDE!"

"Are you cool with –"

"C'mon. I'm good. It all makes sense now too. I suspected, but I figured we needed definite answers to support my hypothesis of why he came over here, after our cardboard, noncommittal, white bread kiss and I'm glad it makes you happy. Can we go watch *Black Mirror* now, please? My parents get weird when I watch it with them, and they'll be home in another hour or two." She bounded off the bed and down the

stairs.

Bryan saw himself in the mirror over her dresser and smiled.

Even if it was going to be trying at times-- who knew how his parents

would respond, he was afraid of what might happen if anyone at school

found out. He would cross that bridge another day. He was happy right

now. He had Ali as his best friend and something with Quentin, whatever

it was, and that was cool enough.

QUALITIES OF A GOOD KISS IN ORDER OF IMPORTANCE:

1. Somebody that wants to kiss me because they like me. I don't want it from some guy whose drunk in a bar and just wants to kiss *some* girl. That's most important.
2. Surprise
3. Sometimes guys take my glasses off. I wear glasses! Why do you need to take them off? This is how I look.
4. I like it when it's an open -mouthed kiss and it doesn't start off with tongue right away.
5. I've never had anyone bite my lip; I wonder if I'd like it.
6. I have to be attracted to the person to begin with... (CR)

1. The right tongue
2. What's he doing with his hands? I like the hands in my hair, or you know on your face.
3. I like it when they hold my face, but not like squeezy. (Like my Bubby does).
4. I like to know that the other person is enjoying it. You know like, if they're opening their eyes once in a while or making little noises—just not long drawn out. Not when their eyes are open the whole time—that's creepy. (CAT)

Enjoy the tongue the most

There is the lip

Saliva—not too much, not too little

There is breath. Can't be bad. (DC)

Moist

It vibrates

Movement

I don't like gaping, foamy kisses.
[It's] Important to know what the other person wants and be able to judge by their movements.
Empathy is my word of the day.
Sometimes it's like someone is afraid to do what the other person wants.
(Frank F.)

Being, feeling safe #1 not ashamed of who I am—I am enough. This person looks at me and sees that I am enough. Probably only something I ever got from my dog.
Now I'm going to go to the shallow end of the pool:
Lips Second, (they have to be sensual) I like full lips. (VB)

Not a lot of spit. That's the first thing I think of cause I'm so romantic. I like it when you're out with someone and they kind of sneak up on you. It's a surprise. I don't like the "I'm going to kiss you now!!!" moment. I like a soft kiss, not a lot of pressure. I don't need your tongue all the way down my throat. On the other hand, if we're not talking about romantic kisses, my three -year- old cousin gives fantastic kisses on the cheek. He's adorable, he'll come and give me a great kiss and say, "I love you!" I love that with all little kids, they're just happy to see you. Like with dogs you can be gone for two minutes or two weeks and they'll come and kiss you and it's so sweet and pure and there's nothing behind it. It's an "I wanna hug you and I wanna kiss you" kind of thing.

I like the slowness of it. I like the softness of it. I don't like it rough. I mean the pressure. Not really hard. I don't mean the person's actual lips. I'm just kind of into slowness. Don't immediately jump in and stick your tongue in. It's nice later on. (CR)

I can tell you what it's not. I don't like big and slobbery—I don't like a lot of saliva and I don't like the over the lip kiss. There's some guys who put both of their lips over your lips, kind of like a squid or something. That hasn't happened in a long time, maybe.

A good kiss should be—not rushed, lingering, should involve other closeness whether it's hands in the hair or the face or the back of your head. Taking your time. Of course I have to like the person. There has to be tongue. You gotta move it around. I don't like the in and out. I like the around. Could be forceful, could be tender. (CAT)

A connection within the kiss. It's not kissing to be clever; it's not kissing to touch. It's kissing cause it's the thing to do. It's like kissing to make the pieces fit. Kisses have to be sacred and passionate and they have to feel good. They can't be forced, but you gotta open up to that kiss. Mamagale taught me that. I love to kiss because of her.

That's what I'm talking about NOW, the best kiss physically. You can taste the texture of a person's feelings. It does transport you because physically it almost makes you separate from everything else but that kiss. It may lead to something else, just momentarily, but you know in that moment that all that matters in that moment is that kiss. It has a certain juiciness to it. It's not dry, but it's not too wet. You match. Your lips match. It doesn't try to take itself out of the moment, it stays in the moment. It lets itself run the course of what it is--and that's how you know cause you wanna do it again. (DC)

Lips together not totally tight, a little bit apart. Someone coming into you and not covering the mouth. I hate a kiss where someone is coming in at you and totally covering your mouth. Kisses have to be good brain sex. (Frank F.)

It has to have levels. It can begin kind of soft and not very intense, sort of delicate and really feeling each other's lips. I think that's important to feel the sensation of lips and then deepen. The pressure gets more and maybe the mouth opens up a little bit. It almost has to have shape to it. It's almost like a song.
You know there's an arc to it.
There are places where the volume of it, if you will, gets turned up. There are places where it backs off a little bit. The rhythm of it needs to ebb and flow and I think you both have to be on the same page about it.
You both have to WANT it.
It's almost as if the kiss itself directs where you'll go. It can't be like one or the other is controlling the intensity. I don't think anyone in a kiss wants to feel as if they're being controlled.
I think it needs to feel organic and you're finding

yourself living from space to space within the kiss.
(Tasha Bell)

A good kiss... is like a great mousse there's a texture to it. When it's really right you really can't imitate it. A good kiss is straight on looking at the person. I do like starting with your eyes open. It starts sweetly, romantically. There's a certain amount of pressure you feel on your lips. It's not forced. It's not one of those raw passionate ones, you know and it's not like your mouth's open immediately. You start there, and then you just kind of—you open your mouth and it lingers and you just gotta be touching. I like to put my hand on the back of someone's head or I hold their face, their chin. If someone does that to me, that kind of makes me go "aaaahhhh."
I'm thinking about the kiss and I may need to go to the bathroom now. (VB)

HAIKU #4
Ocean thunder roars

Your soul and mine connect with kisses

Sand rash spoils the fun

Blowing Off Steam

The music was loud.

The band was pretty good for a knock off, derivative, supposedly blues band that was really playing covers of Huey Lewis and The News, songs that were watered down enormously. The bar was crowded with beer-bellied guys leaning back against the bar, eyes scanning the crowd like hungry animals on the prey. It reminded Ellen of an episode of one of those nature shows like "When Animals Attack." The bar was the bush and all the women were unsuspecting antelopes who needed to be able to run like hell when the time came to save themselves.

"God, I hope I don't look like dinner to any of these guys."

She fought the urge to sniff her underarms just to make sure she wasn't giving off some kind of pheromone invitation by accident. Instead she just focused on the lead singer. He was kind of cute in a watered-down Huey Lewis kind of way. Truthfully, she didn't have anything against Huey Lewis. She actually liked his voice and their songs. This guy's voice was pretty good too. He wasn't Huey, but not bad.

"I'm so cranky" she muttered to herself as she sipped her Belgian beer.

The look the guy at the bar had given her when she'd asked for a Blue Moon—you'd have thought she had three heads. That's what happens in small towns that have one bar with live music, and everybody drinks Bud. Maybe it was due to her nomadic lifestyle that her tastes had moved beyond Bud. Six years in LA, three in Dallas, another three in Philly and then she'd finally settled in New York. Well, she had thought she was settled until she got the call that her mother was sick, and she needed to come back home to help take care of her. Wrong, she corrected herself mentally, to take care of her *by herself* since none of her siblings felt her life meant enough to stay where she was. They had husbands. They had kids. They had jobs. Well so did she, but no one thought her job as a freelance writer was important enough to prevent her from attending to Mom. She only knew this because they'd mentioned it to her several times, each one of them individually, during the frantic phone calls to sort out what they should do *about Mom*. So here she was back in Michigan. Back in the town that called itself a city, but had one bar with live music, three movie theatres, eight malls, two

of which were closing, sitting here listening to "The Power of Love," by

the Huey Lewis knock-off. Now, if it was the real Huey Lewis, this would

be a different story. A very different story. Because she had to admit,

she did like Huey Lewis.

Recently, one night she and her niece Rachel were watching

some YouTube videos because she felt her aunt needed to know who

the best new bands were. Ellen had no idea why. She was fine with her

music, the music of the eighties. She didn't even remember the names of

those bands Rachel showed her, except for the one with that Florence

chick and her Machine. They were pretty cool. Then it was Ellen's turn to

show Rachel what good music really meant. She'd flipped through a few

of her favorite videos from the eighties and one of them was a Huey

Lewis and The News video. He was a hottie back in the day. Rachel had

rolled her eyes and started scrolling through her iPhone.

No taste.

At that moment, the backbeat of "I Want A New Drug," kicked in

and Ellen started thinking about the video they'd watched for this song.

She let her head start bopping, pretty soon that bop was working its way into her shoulders. He wasn't so bad; this knock off guy. He really did kind of look like the real one, circa nineteen eighty-three. His shirt was open so you could see the chest hair poking up out of his button-down shirt, only because he'd left the top two buttons open, very much like the real Huey Lewis.

"These guys are pretty good, huh?"

Some dude in a flannel shirt *jeez, it's July, and he's in a flannel shirt*—was leaning on the back of the unoccupied chair at her table, bottle of Bud in one hand, smiling at her.

"Uhhh, they're okay" Ellen said, in the most disinterested voice she could muster.

"You wait, they're just getting warmed up. Never seen you here before—" and Flannel-Shirt-In-July starts to pull out the chair and sit down.

Awww, hell no!

"Sorry, I'm waiting for someone. He should be here soon."

"Well, he sure is a lucky guy—you can tell him that for me. Hot chick like you left alone for too long, well, you never know, somebody might just snatch you up from him."

"I'll tell him you said so. Have a great night."

He smiled.

Please God, let those brown stains on his teeth be from chewing tobacco and not anything else.

He headed back to the bar and reassumed the leaning back position with the other guys from the town that calls itself a city.

For a moment, Ellen felt a twinge of guilt and regret. She could've let him sit with her, so she'd at least have someone to talk to. It might've been a nice change from the doctors and strained conversations with siblings and the cajoling of her mother to "please Ma, take your medicine." But she knew better. This was not her scene, she just wanted to hear some music, be left alone, let off some steam, and drink her Blue Moon. She didn't want to be bothered. After that exchange she knew this was not her scene. *"Snatched?" Yeah.* She was more than just a touch creeped out.

To be honest Ellen really did want to be bothered, but in a more meaningful way than passing the time with someone who she had no interest in.

And with brown teeth stains.

She wanted to have some interest in someone again. Dammit! Forty-two, single, and no, she was not dying to be married again; that was not the point. Especially since the first one had worked out so well. Dirk had hit forty and turned into a Dick. Deciding that he needed to "experience more of life than I possibly can being married to you. Because face it, hon, you're married to your work."

Really, it was the little dark-haired girl who worked in his office. He was such a cliché.

So yeah, she was bitter, angry and a little bit afraid. Not that she would never get married again, or have a deep relationship again, more that she wouldn't be able to connect again, and have it mean something to her. Connect?

Connect how? I don't even know what the hell that means.

She thought about that and settled on even if it was something as simple as a kiss. How long had it been since she'd had a good kiss?

Like the one in the romance novels she read every now and then. She preferred reading good old-fashioned scary, gothic novels, but she'd run out of her supply for now and she'd started reading the only books her mom had on her bookshelf-- romance novels. The bad kind. With the hunky, impossibly chiseled guys on the cover.

Hey, at least they put me to sleep.

Maybe she should get a library card and check out some Jane Austen or Edith Wharton. They knew how to write about kissing.

"Good Lord woman, you're still thinking about Mr. Darcy at your age?!" she chided herself. Yes, she was. Mr. Darcy, and the kisses she'd had as a teenager. She knew some good kissers back then.

Dirk sucked at kissing, literally and figuratively. That's how she should've known that she and Dirk were not going to make it. He kissed for shit. Teeth bumping, his tongue attacking her like they were doing combat in *Game of Thrones*. There was no joy in those kisses, yet she convinced herself other things were good enough to make it work. Important things to be respected. Like Dirk was financially responsible; he had dreams and goals. He was there when she needed him after she'd gotten hit by a car riding her bike around Manhattan. "What does a kiss really matter?" She was putting too much emphasis on something as stupid as a kiss. She wasn't a kid when she and Dirk-the-Dick had married. She was thirty-two for God's sake. Still, she'd wondered about it, if it would ever get better. For a while she tried to teach him how she liked being kissed. That went well. He got all indignant as he did with most things if someone offered a possibly better or new way to do anything.

"Are you telling me I can't kiss?" he'd huff at her, crossing his arms and legs, becoming impenetrable.

She had wanted his kisses to move her like some of the ones from her past had. Those boys she'd kissed and felt as if the earth had trembled, as if her breath had to be regained because it was so powerful. Not hard kisses. Nor long kisses. And she couldn't name what it possessed if she had to ... you just felt it. You felt it all through your body, down to your soul.

Connection.

She had wanted to say, "Yes, but I can show you what I like." Of course, that would've sent him off into self-righteous, extremely sensitive yelling mode, which you avoided at all costs.

Instead she had said, "No, I'm just thinking we could try some different things," in her sweet, bullshit voice. The one she used to get him to do anything outside of his norm, which was about ninety percent of everything.

God, I am still so bitter.

She shook her head, clearing it of the memory. Trying to clear it of all the crap rolling around inside of her. She wanted to be back in New York where there were all kinds of things to do! Fun things, music, theatre, museums, more than one bar with a band. Even though someone had the bright idea that New York should be as homogenous as the rest of the world, they couldn't completely make it that way, and for that she was grateful. New York was different than this. Better than this. But this was what she had for now; she had to make the best of it.

The band was launching into a Van Morrison song. Ellen made the commitment to enjoy the music and have a good time even if it was, she checked her phone...

Cripe! It's only nine o'clock. I've only been here thirty-two minutes.

"Alright," she told herself. "I'll stay for another thirty minutes before heading back to the house." As soon as she finished this beer, she'd order another Blue Moon and relish the look on the guy's face when she ordered it. Why not have another? She was taking a Lyft so no worries about driving. The deal was set leave after the second beer.

Yeah, I had a couple of beers and listened to music. Great night out! She would be happy with that. At this point, this was the best she could hope for while "out on the town" in this little town that called itself a city.

With the firm resolution of having a good time she began to bop again and sipped the remainder of her almost lukewarm Blue Moon.

Maybe it was all that thinking about how awful it was to kiss Dirk that reminded her that she hadn't had a good kiss, *a really good kiss*, in a long, long time. That was the exact moment "Huey Lewis Light" looked at her and smiled. Completely caught her off guard. Okay, so he had a nice smile. Along with that nice smile, he had nice lips, and she began to wonder what it would be like to kiss those lips.

"Wow, Ellen, you are losing your shit. Get a grip girl," she chastised

herself.

Out loud she muttered, "Get a fucking grip."

Then she looked around to see if anyone heard her. That's when Flannel-Shirt-In-July raised his Bud bottle to her in a silent salute. She realized this would be the moment to get some fresh air. Right now. She'd go outside and call to check on her mom. One of the neighbors, Kate, was sitting with her until midnight so Ellen could have a breather after three weeks of being there, doing the shopping, handling the doctor visits, and just being there all the time. But she should call. What kind of daughter would she be if she didn't call? She turned to the table next to her and asked a girl in a midriff top and tight, ripped jeans, who resembled a red- headed Bratz doll, big eyes, big hair, pouty mouth, tiny waist and all-- if she'd watch her table, promising she'd be right back. She responded by giving Ellen a thumbs-up.

She slipped out the door, walking towards the parking lot, and could still hear the bass and drums of the band booming outside. Ellen was tempted to call her Lyft and just go, tell Kate to go home and she'd spend the night watching something on demand again. But she hadn't been out in three weeks and she was finding herself being short and impatient with her mom the past few days. She really needed to blow off some steam. She didn't have a gym membership here-- couldn't afford one because she was parceling out her money until the checks for the last few articles and stories she'd written came in from the publishers. This was the best way to release she could think of. Go inside listen to the music, maybe dance—that would blow off some steam. Stop thinking about Dirk and the siblings and New York and the shit that made her sad. She felt the sting of tears but willed herself not to cry. After all, she'd made herself a promise of a fresh Blue Moon, and she wasn't about to walk back in there tear-streaked for Huey Lewis Light, Flannel Shirt, and the Living Bratz Doll to see. Especially Flannel Shirt-- God no! That might motivate him to come back over to comfort her. That was the last thing she wanted.

"Hey Kate, how's Mom?"

"She's good. Sleeping for the past twenty minutes or so. How are you? Having a good time?"

"Oh yeah," she lied, "It's going gangbusters."

"Oh no! There's a gang where you are?"

"No, Kate. A figure of speech. I'm having a great time."

"Oh, you writers and your fancy words. Well you just stay out as long as you like. You deserve it. Have the best time ever."

"Do my best. Hey, if you or Mom need me just call, okay? I won't be out too much longer anyway."

"Don't you worry about us. We're just fine. Go ahead and have a great time. I'm sure you are living it up."

"Yeah, like you can't even imagine. I'll see you soon."

She disconnected.

Well, that's that. I've got to stay out a little bit longer otherwise they'll both be questioning me to death about why I'm home so early and I just can't.

Checking her face in the side view mirror of one of the parked cars in the lot, she made sure there were no mascara streaks. She noticed that her grey hairs seemed prolific; even though she'd tried to dye them, they always came back with a vengeance. The lines on her forehead and around her almond-shaped eyes were getting deeper. It had taken her into her thirties to stop regretting that her eyes were brown and not blue like her mom's. She didn't look that bad. She'd dye her hair again this week and find some kind of miracle cream and--

Nope, stop it. Accept the fact that you're aging. Here you are with a head full of gray hair and you're thinking about a mythical kiss. You are in such great shape. Note to self, maybe find a therapist here so you can get your shit together.

She made a deal with herself, dance one dance, finish the beer, and then call for a Lyft.

For five minutes just enjoy yourself, forget about everything else, and just have fun. Who knows, maybe five minutes will turn into ten or twenty, and you need that, Ellen. You need to have some fun before you completely turn into a bitter bitchy old broad.

As she was going in through the first set of double doors leading in and out of the bar, somebody was coming out the second, interior door quickly with a phone to his ear.

"Sorry, excuse me" he pushed past her "What are you talking about man I didn't—" then the door closed, and he was gone.

Ellen called out "Asshole," as she slipped back into the bar.

She ordered her second beer and gave the bartender a cold stare as he smirked, while telling her the waitress would bring it over to her since she was sitting at a table now.

Yeah, I ordered a Blue Moon. Fight me.

Red-headed Bratz smiled when she returned to her table and gave her another thumbs-up. "I thought you weren't coming back. Like three people tried to like take that table. They were really like aggressive, ya know? But I stood up for you sister." And she raised her hand for a high five. Ellen obliged with a tight smile.

"Sorry 'bout that—had to make a call. Thanks. Let me buy you a beer for your trouble."

"Nah, it's okay. My man's got me covered."

"My man" oh I'm so happy for you.

She immediately made an apology to the universe.

I can't keep being this ornery.

The band was starting up with another song, something from the eighties. *Well, at least it's my music,* Ellen thought. She began mentally preparing herself to get up and dance with or without a partner when the right song came on.

"*You can do this. Man, or no man*" she repeated in her head over and over again.

The waitress brought her new beer over, and Ellen took a huge drink, steeling herself for what was next. The moment she would risk it all. "*God this is like high school again,*" she couldn't help thinking. Back when nobody asked her to dance so she'd go on the gymnasium floor and dance by herself in this small town that called itself a city—and there was NEVER a band at school dances. Actually, she'd even had to do it a few times as an adult when she came back to the town that wasn't a city but wanted to be, in her twenties, and went out on her own. All of her friends from school were either married with kids or she couldn't find them, so she went out on her own. Always. Always she ended up sitting alone in some bar trying to enjoy herself and it always was a let-down. At least this time there was a band that played pretty good music.

It was always sad and depressing, and each time she visited she'd swear never to return, or if she did it would be for two or three days only. Not long enough for her and her mother to get into one of their many fights causing Ellen to bolt out the door seeking some refuge in a bar. Cause what else was there?

Yet, here I am again.

In a bar. The only bar with a band.

The band began to play yet another Huey Lewis and the News song, "It's Hip To Be Square." Ellen figured this was good enough to do her five minutes of release. She took a swig and just as she was pushing her chair back someone bumped into her.

"Hey, sorry."

He was tall, tan, with long straight hair. He wasn't tan, he was golden or, what? She didn't know, except that he was gorgeous.

"I wanted to apologize for bumping into you out there."

"No worries."

"It was an asshole move. I had to deal with this jerk, I'm sorry. Let me buy you beer to make up for it."

What is this? The universal language of apology here, is "Let me buy you a beer"?

From this guy she wouldn't mind though. He was truly beautiful in an unconventional way. His face was almost round, but the cheek bones were just significant enough to stop the roundness. He was a golden-brown color and his eyes were a strange mix of hazel and gray, which created an almost hypnotic effect.

"Seriously no worries," she said.

"Not worried about a worry, but I pulled an asshole move—at least that's what you said—and I need to make up for that."

Ellen blushed. "You heard that?"

"Good ears." He smiled one of the most dazzling and at the same time warm smiles she'd ever seen.

She smiled back while her mind raced around like a pinball banging off the walls.

You can shut this down or at least have some conversation. Maybe you should just go—My God he is gorgeous. Calm down Ellen.

All of this as she saw Flannel Shirt-in-July staring. Well, if she told this guy to get lost, he might want to come back over and she definitely wasn't interested in him. As if that wasn't enough, Huey Lewis Light seemed to be staring at her. She wondered if her boob had fallen out or something. Why were all these guys suddenly paying attention to her?

"How about that beer?" he asked, leaning closer.

He smelled good. It was a light musk, but not too sweet. She realized that she was sitting there mute, staring at him. She snapped out of it.

"Sure. Thanks."

"What are you drinking?"

"Blue Moon, but you know, really, you don't have to I just ordered this one—"

"Yeah, but we can have a drink together now. I mean, if you don't mind." He walked away towards the bar before she could answer.

What are you doing? You don't want to be bothered—you need to leave, right now!

She considered grabbing her purse and slipping out while his back was turned, but then she remembered her promise to herself. *Five minutes of dancing, let off the steam, and then go home so you can be a kind, relaxed person again with Mom.* So, she sat back in the chair and took a few deep breaths. When he returned, he had two beers.

"I never tried this Blue Moon stuff. It's pretty good. Kind of light. You drink this all the time?"

"Usually. Thanks."

Awkward!

Just silence. It was a big fucking long silence. Within that silence Ellen could swear she heard a meteor hurtling towards the earth about to smash into the bar, right where she was sitting. She looked at him. He at her.

SAY SOMETHING! You need to SAY SOMETHING! This is worse than high school! Has it really been that damn long since you've interacted with a hot guy?

He leaned towards her, shouting over the music. She could smell that damn musk again. "Never seen you here before."

"I don't live here anymore—"

"Oh, so you used to? Why in the fuck would you come back here? Not the most exciting place in the world."

She laughed. "Yeah, I know."

"There's like three dive bars here and they like trade off what nights they're open and man this is the only place with a band. Tell ya, one day I'm gonna leave here. Don't know where I'll go, but I figure I've got time to figure it out."

Christ! How old is he? "I've got time?"

As if he read her mind, "I'll be twenty-six next month. Just working, getting some money together so I can book out of here. Helping my mom out, you know? So, what is it?"

Completely confused, Ellen looked at him, dazzled by his eyes, and that wide, beautiful smile, "What?"

"Brings you back here?"

"I… I'm helping with some family stuff."

"Okay. Cool. So, where have ya been living when you're not here?"

"I've moved around a lot, you know, living different places."

His eyes lit up, a bigger, brighter smile, "Yeah? Like where?"

"Dallas, L.A. Philly and New York—so far—"

"Whoaaa, that is so major cool. "

Did he really say, "major cool?" Aw damn. He is a kid and I need to go home. I just need to leave now—

"Hey you wanna dance? I love this song. This band's okay, they play the same shit, but I like them."

It was a Bowie song, "Modern Love."

Before Ellen could decide, he'd pulled her onto the floor. They found a space off to the side.

He yelled over the song, "I don't dance so good, but I love to dance."

And they danced. They danced through three or four songs. Midway through the second song, Ellen felt something release. She closed her eyes and let the music take her away. She wasn't thinking about her mother or siblings, or about how she was going to pay the credit card bills that were waiting on the next check. She was just with the music and she didn't care if the band was great or not. As long as she could find the beat, she was gone. She didn't care that when she opened her eyes every now and then Huey Lewis Light was looking at her or that Flannel-Shirt-in-July was glaring at her. She just didn't care.

They played a Prince song, badly, but it had a beat and she was happy.

Half-way through "Moondance," the guy, him—

Christ I don't even know his name—

Was close to her—not touching her, but it felt good. She looked

at him. His eyes were focused on her. Gently, he placed his hand on her

shoulder and she moved right into him. Effortlessly they were moving

together easily, smoothly. Ellen felt another release. A release she'd

been holding onto for a long time. She let her guard down and moved

closer to him. They were breathing together.

Moving together.

Without thinking, she put her arms around his waist. She felt his

breath warm on her neck. It was so good.

The song ended.

"We're taking a short break. Be back in a few. Don't go

anywhere," Huey Lewis Light was saying.

The guy, she had to ask his name at some point, smiled at her and

took a step back. Something about that step back made her a little hungry inside. Made something ache within her.

"I haven't danced like that in a while. You dance really good."

"You're a good partner." She smiled at him. She wanted to say more but didn't know what to say because she was chiding herself: *He's twenty-five for Christ sakes, Ellen!*

"It's hot in here. You want to go outside get some air?"

"Yeah, sure." Her shirt was sweaty and sticking to her. She was hoping he wouldn't ask her to smoke. She didn't smoke and wouldn't since she'd seen what it had done to her mom.

They both paused at the table to take sips of their tepid beer. "Damn, kind of warm. We'll just do this, so we don't lose our table" He put the paper coasters on top of both glasses. "We'll get fresh when we come back. Okay?"

"Sure, my treat this time."

As they were walking towards the door, she noticed Huey Lewis Light sitting at a nearby table with a group of people. He smiled at her. Ol' Flannel-Shirt-in-July raised his glass in a silent toast.

Once outside with--*You need to ask him his name*-- the air felt

crisp. Ellen could swear that it was almost electric. *Wow, how corny?*
You've written better than this while hungover and writhing in pain. But it
did feel electric, full of little currents of anticipation. It was like they'd
taken the connection from the dance floor to outside where there was
space for it to grow and fill them both to the point of satisfaction.

"It was good dancing together. You dance really good. Are you
having a good time?" he leaned forward and tilted his head, so his hair
fell across his left eye, which made him even more sexy than before.

Sexy? Sexy, when did THAT enter the equation?! Okay, yeah, sooo
he's sexy. He's sexy, he's hot, he's YOUNG, Ellen! And he is beautiful.

"Yes, I am having a really good time. You know—" and before
she could ask him his name, he put both arms on her shoulders and
pulled her close.

"Yeah, me, too. Are you staying in town for a while?"

"I don't kn—I mean, well it looks like it."

"Good, cause maybe we could hang out again. There's not much
to do here, but I'm sure we could find something to keep us busy."

Those words painted pictures in Ellen's mind. Her imagination bursting with the thought of what it would be like to have time with him as an alternative to the stress and sadness made her stomach do a little vibration. She would and could blow off some serious steam with-- *What the hell is his name? Did he tell me, and I forgot? I have to ask*—

"Yeah, like. I dig older chicks."

Really? Okay yes, I am older, but damn you don't just—

"I mean older chicks know what they're doing and all. I'd like to get to know you, you know, if that's like cool with you?"

What the hell? I'm here. I'm bored. He's gorgeous and it ain't love, Ellen. It wouldn't be love, but lust is not to be discounted, and I AM older.

Ellen decided to take the bull by the horns and leaned in to go for a kiss. Afterall she's the "older chick" by about seventeen years. *If he's willing so am I.*

Just then there was an odor.

A disgusting, ripe, putrid odor.

"Oh damn. Sorry about that. I think it's that fancy beer. Don't think my gut can handle it." He fanned the air around them as he moved.

He farted?! We were in an embrace. I was going in for a kiss and he farted!! Then he moved away?!!

Suddenly the images transformed into moment after moment of her jumping out bed gagging or fanning noxious odors away or standing in some anonymous bathroom, spraying can after can of air freshener. There were other images of her dealing with him doing dumb, young shit. This was not the release she needed.

"Wow, don't know what's wrong with me. Sorry—"

He did it again! Seriously?!!!

She was attempting to think of a way to get out of this without it turning into an ugly argument about you just don't do that when his cell phone rang.

"Hey! What?! No man, I said—" He mouthed, "I'll be back," and took off around the corner leaving remnants of his aromatic destruction behind him.

Ellen decided it was time to leave. Enough was enough. This night had been a total bust.

Should've left well enough alone and had my beer, danced by myself, then left. That would've been fine, but noooo.

She began to walk down the street, thinking it would be better to have the Lyft pick her up somewhere else. There was a 7-Eleven down the street. She could pick up snacks to fortify her while she found something to binge watch on Netflix for the rest of the night.

Another lovely night here in the town that thinks it's a city.

As she started to cross the street someone stepped next to her. She looked up and into the eyes of Huey Lewis Light.

He smiled at her. "Hey, don't tell me you're going home already?"

"What? Oh, yeah, need to get back. I'm just here visiting. My mother's not well and…"

"Sorry to hear that. I hope she gets better."

"It's not looking great, but you know the doctors are doing what they can. Sometimes you just have to be patient—can't give up hope, you know?" *Why am I blathering?*

"Absolutely. Brandon."

"Oh, Ellen. Good to meet you. You guys sound great."

He was not as tall up close, and she hadn't noticed the gray in his hair while he was playing with the band.

"You caught us on a good night." And he laughed. His dimples were just like the real Huey Lewis. "Are we going the same way?"

"7-eleven?"

"Yep. Sometimes a man just needs a little chocolate to get through the night."

Ellen laughed as they crossed the street and entered the store, "Now, that's something I've never heard."

They separated as she went on her mission for chips, seltzer, and yes, some chocolate. They ran into each other again at the cash register. They stood there in silence. Ellen contemplating what to binge on tonight again.

Brandon held the door for her as they left. "Hey, if you're going to be in town for a while I hope you'll come back around. We're here every Thursday night."

"I'll try. I don't get out much—with my mother and all, but I'll try."

She had called for her Lyft to meet her here and it said about three minutes away.

"You meeting someone here?"

"Yeah, my Lyft. I didn't want to drive in case I had too much to drink."

"Smart." And there was a pause as he shifted around and played with the bag containing his chocolate bars. "Say, I know this sounds weird, but I really do hope you come back—I mean, I saw you dancing and listening to the music and I don't know-- I just—I hope you come back. You seemed like you were having a good time—"

"I was—I did. Like I said you guys sound great—"

"Thanks, but I mean, like you—I don't—man, this is going to sound so weird. Sometimes you can, you know like get a … a vibe or a feeling off of people and you just seem like good people. Like free and comfortable and—shit, I'm talking too much—"

Ellen smiled, really smiled. "Really? Thanks. That's another thing that's new." And she remembered the days when she had felt free and comfortable in her skin and realized that's what she'd been trying to get back to since, when? Since she had returned to take care of her mother?

Since her marriage-- or the divorce from Dirk? All she knew was it had been a long time since she'd felt really free enough to be herself, to not second guess herself, to just do. It had been so long since she'd not felt like she was in a cage constructed of all her limitations. Released.

She stared at Brandon and wanted to cry and wanted to laugh. A dark blue sedan, her Lyft, pulled up in the parking lot.

"That's my ride."

"Hey, have a good night Ellen. Enjoy your chocolate. It was good talking to you." He walked with her to the car and opened the door.

Ellen didn't hesitate, didn't think.

"It's been cool meeting you, too."

She kissed him on the cheek. For two seconds that felt like twenty minutes her lips lingered a quarter of an inch from his cheek. He turned to look at her and they kissed. It was less than a minute, but Ellen felt something move in her.

Get a--

The thought never finished because she was moved from earth to sky she was soaring through air, her skin tingled, her breath caught.

She felt warm all over. She sighed and heard Brandon sigh at the same time. She opened her eyes and they both laughed. It wasn't awkward laughter it was shared.

He placed a hand on her shoulder. "Yeah. Come back, will ya?"

"Yeah." And she knew she meant it. She got into the Lyft and he closed the door. As the driver pulled away, she looked back, and he was standing there smiling. Ellen smiled.

BEST KISS YOU EVER HAD?

There've been a few. Well there was this one guy. We were friends in high school. I liked him and he liked me, but – and to this day I'm kind of dumb about these things—cause I'm kind of a tomboy—I don't understand that they like me like that. "Oh wait you're kissing me! Whoa, whoa- whoa!"— Anyway, in high school we'd hang out but either he was dating someone, or I was dating someone. Many years went past, then we reconnected. So we started flirting and flirting and flirting. We decided to go out and now we're grown-ups and so... I kind of expected that something was going to happen, wasn't sure what. We met in the middle of the day. We'd said we'd go for a late lunch. I hadn't seen him in person in a while, it was either on the phone or email [we talked]. When we got together I was like, "Oh, he is pretty cute." We had lunch. He said, "Let's go someplace for drinks." We were walking to his car and he says, "Oh hold on for a minute." And I was like, "What?" He grabbed my hand, I thought something was wrong. He whipped me around and laid one on me and I was like wow! Cause it was suave and unexpected in the way he did it. It was just a really good kiss. I think because there had been all this build up and expectation in my mind. It was slow, lingering, romantic. (CAT)

I was turning 11, so there were these girls that moved down from Mississippi to Ithaca and there was some disaster that had happened in MS. For some reason there were a lot of people in Ithaca from MS. I don't know what was happening. There was this one girl [we'll call her M] she was more developed that the other girls. She said to me one time, "Have you ever been kissed?" and I said "Yeah! I kiss all the time." She was like, "Let me see!" and she pulled into some corner and she put her tongue in my mouth. At first she was like "Open your mouth!" and I was like, "Oh!" I opened my mouth and her tongue was so juicy she was like, "Let me feel your tongue!" and that was so juicy, and she was like, "Don't you ever let me hear about you kissing somebody without getting some tongue!" and I was like, "Let's do it again." And I think we must've kissed for like an hour straight. She must've been thirteen. Anybody I have been with says that I am a good kisser and that's because "M." taught me you have to kiss like you mean it. (DC)

It's definitely about the mouth for me. I can look at someone's mouth and be like: I WANT TO KISS THEM. It's like looking at a piece of cheesecake, you know when you want it and you know when it's dry.

It depends on where you're at that makes a good or a bad kiss. If I think about it, some of my better kisses have been unanticipated. I didn't expect it and it was like, "Oooo, that was nice. Really nice." It shifts my mental gears. There's a really old - fashioned respect around this. Not like somebody [literally] asks can I kiss you. It's like that energy that I think someone gets when the time is right. I feel like you both can feel that and *you're kind of in sync. It's just an unspoken respect. I'm asking and you're approving or you're asking and I'm approving. Because kissing is very intimate emotionally. It may be the core of what I want. (VB)*

I thought this guy was my ideal. I had broken off a seven- year relationship.
It was simple it wasn't forced. It was like little [movements], but one of us moved forward and the other moved back. It lasted about an hour, it went on and on. A lot of lips, peripheral tongue- not down the throat, a little bit in the mouth.
Instant erection. That kiss was AMAZING. (Frank F.)

Haiku #5

Apricot nectar

Your lips seeking an answer

Frozen ponds await

AND WHAT ABOUT YOU?

WHAT ARE THE QUALITIES OF A GOOD KISS TO YOU?

WHAT DO YOU REMEMBER ABOUT YOUR FIRST KISS?

WHAT IS THE WORST THING SOMEONE CAN DO WHILE KISSING YOU? (TOO MUCH TONGUE, BITING? OPEN EYES OR CLOSED)?

THE GAME

Nelson's mind was screaming at him, "Whose idea was this anyway?! How did I end up here?" He paused as he realized, "Shit, it was mine. My really brilliant idea!"

It had begun with the party. It was Charmaine's party for her fortieth birthday. Charmaine, who looked like she was twenty-five if a day. Gorgeous Charmaine, who was married to Lindsay. What a couple they made. Charmaine with her voluminous, curly afro, deep brown skin, and banging bod—even though she was short, she had legs that seemed to take up her entire body, which was generously curvy. Then there was Lindsay, with her massive head of curly red hair, and milky, pale skin that did not contain one wrinkle. She was tall and thin, but she emanated strength. You didn't mess with Lindsay. They were both perfect in every way a human specimen could be. Just like everyone else who was sitting around at the party. Nelson didn't include himself in that idea of physical perfection, but he was okay. He was maybe even a little bit better than okay at five ten, with jet-black hair that he'd recently cut stylishly short, but long enough to still look a little edgy. He chose to accent his gray eyes with dark rimmed glasses, even though he really didn't need them, but he believed they made him look like he was knowledgeable and sophisticated. Because of his very square jawline people often assumed he was some dumb jock-- he hated it when people treated him like he was shallow. Hence the glasses, which were a device to encourage them to look beyond the jawline and, hopefully, realize how deep he really was. It was all part of his strategy to winning the game. To tell the truth, he was doing better than okay when it came to other things as well.

At thirty-eight he was settled into a great job working on Wall Street. The kind of job that when he told people what he did, within three minutes their eyes glazed over. He didn't care. Glaze all you want he always thought, because he was making money, more money than he could've ever imagined he would when he was younger and had just moved to New York City. Family and friends back in Wisconsin had warned him the big bubble of the eighties had burst, and he was going into the wrong business. Maybe some of those bubbles had burst, but Nelson was confidently and securely ensconced in one that just seemed to keep rising. He had recently purchased a one bedroom on the Upper West Side, a full one bedroom, not some weird half-assed space. It had been over a decade since Nelson had needed a roommate to help augment his income. It had been five years since he'd moved from Queens to Manhattan. He could've moved to Brooklyn, but the whole L train disaster seemed to be looming ahead. He'd heard the rumors, which he had listened to, so he was prepared when the line had started undergoing delays and all that other madness two weeks ago. He had to restrain himself tonight from gloating when he'd overheard several guests complaining about their daily commutes to Manhattan or Queens for work. Nelson hardly ever had to travel to Brooklyn, tonight was the exception. He was glad for that, and he gloated silently, which was allowed.

Nelson leaned against the bar and did what he was naturally good at doing in preparing to win the game: surveying the landscape and making wise choices. It was all part of how he always succeeded. He'd functioned like this for so many years, it was just habit now, natural, like breathing. First there's observation, then listening to pick up clues and pertinent information, and finally there was follow-through

to make sure things happened the way he wanted them to every time.

Yet, the most important thing was timing. It was the thing you couldn't

predict. You just had to know when to make your move, put in your bid,

hold your tongue, or say just the right thing. He'd been lucky so far.

That's how he'd scored his new apartment. One day he noticed

one of his colleagues at work, Joey, was upset and angry. Then he heard

the stories from others about him fighting to avoid being kicked out of

his apartment. He'd listened as Joey complained about the landlord

trying to kick people out. Then Nelson waited and surveyed the website

Joey had mentioned that held the tenants' complaints and information

about the subsequent lawsuit that followed against the landlord. The

tenants had lost. Nelson had won by swooping in and getting the first

apartment that went onto the market after everyone in the building had

been forced to move. Now he was paying less than anyone else who had

moved in after him. Observing, listening, follow through, and most

definitely timing.

Nelson's timing had also been perfect when his colleague Jim and his wife Regina were going through a divorce. He'd been able to make the right move when she was in that window of not wanting to get serious with anyone but was looking for uncommitted sex. Lots of uncommitted sex, in one night. Actually, his timing had been crucial in this situation. He'd run into her at a bar with some friends while they were having a Divorce Party, with cake, champagne, and gifts—the whole nine. He didn't know people did that, but lucky for him they did. Nelson remembered thinking how badly she must've really wanted out of the relationship to have such an extensive celebration. He watched as she and her friends partied with abandon. He listened as she complained about Jim and all the ways he'd made her angry. By the next morning he'd become part of her divorce party. Neither of them pretended it was anything more than what it was: sex.

As he took in everything happening around him at the party, he smiled remembering that night. Since then, he hadn't seen much action. There weren't many opportunities for him to meet anyone until the invitation to this party. Maybe, one of Lindsay or Charmaine's "sexually fluid," friends could possibly be interested in an older-attractive-although-not-gorgeous-guy with money, a cool apartment, who is upwardly mobile. Why not? As long as they understood he wasn't really interested in a long-term relationship. He had GOALS. They didn't include him getting caught up in some boring, by-the-book relationship that could distract him from his GOALS. However, something for a few weeks or days with great sex would be perfect for him and he was sure there was someone here who fit the bill or at least close enough to make it worth his while. Nelson had planned his look for the night very carefully: jeans with a well-placed single rip, a light blue V-neck sweater that contrasted with his hair, complimented his eyes, and was tight enough to show off his physique. Listening and timing, but none of that mattered if you weren't prepared to step in when it all came together. It was like being called off the bench to get in the game and you didn't have your sneakers. Nelson was prepared, he had his sneakers, and was waiting to get into the game tonight.

As he surveyed the outdoors and indoors, he noticed there were a number of women present. It was clear some of them wouldn't be interested in him since they had dates, but there were a couple that he felt might be a good bet. He was waiting for his moment, when the

timing would be just right, and then all it would take was follow through.

Nelson's smile transformed into a dreamy façade as he surveyed all the

possibilities, looking through the sliding glass doors into the backyard at

the women sitting on the wicker chairs around the fire pit, the pool, and

standing around in small groups talking. There were some guys here, but

he wasn't worried. He wasn't trying to meet all the women, just one.

"Dreaming of the beach, Nelson?" His thoughts were interrupted

by Marcus Lawrence who he knew casually from his early days in New

York and who now worked with Lindsay.

"What?"

"You've got this far away smile on your face. Lindsay told me you

spend a lot of time at the beach—so you know-- or maybe I'm just trying

to start a conversation so I'm not standing around looking like a dork all

night--"

"Oh. Well, yeah, I do, every chance I get. Love it. How're you

doing, man? Haven't seen you since their ten-year anniversary shindig."

"I'm good for the most part. Working long hours, but that's what we've gotta do, right? Getting a little paunchy, though. Old man's gut-"

"Yeah, well you're not alone in that."

Nelson was being kind because Marcus did have a paunch. They were around the same height, but Marcus always seemed to be slouching so he looked shorter than Nelson. He wore his dark brown hair in a very conservative, business cut, and his brown eyes blended in with his olive skin. Nelson almost felt sorry for Marcus, but he didn't have time for that because he was focused on surveying the crowd.

Marcus poured more red wine into his glass, raised the bottle to Nelson, "More?" Nelson nodded, "Bullshit. Look at you. What're you doing? Living at the gym?"

Nelson laughed, "I wish. More like living at work all day, but I do use a standing desk now and sometimes my boss lets me use her Nordic desk."

"Her what?"

He took a long swallow of his wine before he said, "It's a desk with a treadmill attached, so you can get your workout in while you're working. It's amazing. I may not be *living* at the gym, but I do try to get in there at least four times a week." It was his mission to fight aging as much as he could. Forty kind of scared him.

"Oooo kay, man. Four days huh? That's impressive—"

Charmaine inserted herself between them, "What's going on with you two? Being a little anti-social are we?"

Nelson smiled, "Naw, just catching up. We haven't seen each other in a while. By the way, happy birthday!"

Marcus poured more wine into all of their glasses, "Yeah, happy birthday, Char!"

"We're all outside. Come on and hang out with us. Let's all catch up together. Marcus doesn't get to have all the Nelson fun!" Charmaine grabbed his hand leading Nelson outside through the sliding glass doors.

Now this was something to aspire to, he thought as he looked around at the back of their townhouse. Yes, they were out in Brooklyn, so the commute must be killer, but he thought, it had to be worth it to live like this, as he took in the spacious backyard, the firepit ablaze, and all the deep couches encircling it with guests scattered here and there. Although, he noted that the group had thinned dramatically since he'd arrived, there were still quite a few people hanging around. Originally there were about forty, maybe fifty people here. Now it had dwindled to perhaps fifteen or so, sipping wine and talking.

That was the moment Nelson saw her. He hadn't noticed her earlier while he was in the house. Maybe she was a late arrival or had been in another part of the townhouse. Afterall, they had like four bedrooms for Christ sakes. GOALS, he thought. Nelson couldn't tell how old she was, but she was stunning. Her curly, golden brown hair reached just to her nape, her eyes were wide, and in the light of the fire he wasn't sure of the color, but they seemed to be green, or maybe gray, fringed with thick long lashes --not the store-bought ones, either. She was folded into a corner of the couch; it looked like she had long, long legs and he could tell she was lean. The silky tank top she wore revealed sinewy, muscular arms. She appeared to be almost golden in color, but that could've been the fire. Her lips were striking. They were so full and almost heart shaped. They looked soft, like pillows. The kind of lips that he fantasized about in the mornings when he was doing the sinful deed—sometimes he just needed a little jump start to get him going.

Her eyes and lips together alone could equal the end of mankind. All those pieces put together and she looked like a blazing hot Betty Boop. He quickly took the only open space in the seating area, which was diagonally across from her. He spoke to everyone he knew as he joined the group. With her being the only one he didn't know; it gave him a chance to speak to her.

"Nelson." He offered his hand.

She delicately laid hers in his, "Caitlin. Nice to meet you." She quickly looked away.

"Right back atcha." He was confused as to whether she was disinterested in only him or the party.

Without anything more to say unless he wanted to sound like a dork, he sat down and nursed his wine, while occasionally sending a relaxed smile her way, which she ignored. The fire felt good and smelled nice. Something about a fire always relaxed him. His mind drifted to thoughts about the end of summer. The things he wished he'd done. Maybe go on at least one date during those months. He recalled the things he'd tried for the first time and discovered that he loved, like surfing. Riding the waves out in the Rockaways was a new kind of freedom that he really enjoyed. It was challenging, too. Nelson loved being challenged. He looked up and noticed Caitlin staring in the fire, seemingly in an entirely different dimension, another world. She was so beautiful; he became lost in studying her.

He didn't realize that he'd been focusing on her until he heard, "Earth to Nelson. Wow! See? My point exactly!" in Lindsay's soft southern drawl. She threw her head back and laughed, "Let this be a lesson to all of us—get yourselves some down time people! Look at you, Nelson! This is the thing Char and I were just talking about, how we all work so hard that whenever we get a moment to chill, we end up zoning out instead of being present. I submit for everyone's approval: Nelson and Caitlin."

This surprised and pleased Nelson that he and Caitlin were being put together even if it was only in some random conversation.

"What are you talking about?" he said smiling his warmest smile, as he made a point of catching Caitlin's eye.

Marcus grinned, "Exactly that!" and everyone laughed with him.

Nelson began to feel his mood shifting. He hated not being included in the conversation yet, knowing he was the center of it at the same time, and maybe not in a good way—"Which is exactly what?" His voice was almost too strident. Maybe he'd had too much wine.

Charmaine softly laughed, "Nothing bad, Nelson. Relax. Lindsay was just saying how we've all reached that age where we've forgotten how to have simple, innocent fun. We've forgotten how to relax because every waking moment we're thinking about what's next. Trying to quickly attain what we don't have yet, before we're too old—then it ends up being too late to appreciate it."

Lindsay chimed in, "Yeah, we wake up and go to sleep being in the next thing and don't enjoy the present thing. Checking our phones for what's next. On our laptops, searching, without ever seeing what's already here. We spend our time missing 'the present moment.' All of us," she added pointedly.

Nelson relaxed and reached for his wine glass. "Well… yeah, that goes without saying. I always feel like I'm thinking about what I should've done, or I have to do next. It's almost required of us today.

You know? That's the price you pay to stay in the game."

There was a resounding chorus of support around the fire. Nelson felt like he was in control of the situation again as he settled back into his corner of the couch and threw a quick glance and a warm smile in Caitlin's direction. She looked at him and then away quickly.

Marcus spoke up, "Yeah... it almost makes me nostalgic for my youth. Almost."

Another almost perfect woman, with dark brown hair in a pixie cut and large dark eyes and amber skin spoke up. Nelson thought her name was Geneva, "I wouldn't want to go back to my teen years again. They were awful! But... yeah... I do remember that feeling of freedom and, yeah, being present to everything happening-"

Marcus interrupted, "Without commitments and responsibilities—"

Geneva continued, "Yes! None of that—"

Lindsay shook her head as she said, "Kids today don't know what they're missing. Too distracted. Things were far from perfect, but damn I had a good time y'all."

"I do remember some of the crazy things I did back then, but I swear, I cannot remember how I felt doing them—that was so long ago," Charmaine said sadly, as she sipped her wine.

"Oh no. We are not doing any kind of a nostalgia inspired pity party tonight people!" Lindsay chided everyone and they all laughed. "This is a celebration!"

"Seriously though, can anyone remember what it was like to party back then? When we were like fifteen, sixteen?" Marcus asked

There were groans and laughter followed by silence as everyone sipped their wine.

"Well, hell—we're not dead people. C'mon now," Lindsay said. She got up and retrieved another bottle of wine from the tall, glass topped table behind them that was holding several bottles. "What I remember is spending a lot of time being so wasted at parties-- that I can't remember exactly what I did back then—" She began to open the bottle.

"What age are you talking about?" Caitlin asked.

Lindsay paused, "Damn, I can't remember." Everyone laughed,

"That's how wasted I was."

"At sixteen?" Geneva asked.

"Hell yeah! Hey, I lived in a small town in Alabama. Wasn't much else to do."

Caitlin, unfurled from the chair to hold her glass out for Lindsay to fill it, "Okay, how about we pick an age, any age--"

Nelson was right. She was lean from top to bottom. He apologized to the gods of political correctness for objectifying the hell out of her, but he couldn't help it.

Andrew, who was just too damn good looking for his own good—Nelson believed he was bi-racial, Asian and Black, with dark, straight short cropped hair, green eyes, and cheekbones that Nelson was undeniably jealous of; you could tell he worked out a lot-- joined the circle, sitting cross-legged on the ground. "Any age for what?"

Charmaine explained what they'd been talking about as Lindsay filled glasses with one bottle and then opened another.

"Oh, I get it. Nostalgia—and what were we doing at that age?" Andrew asked.

"More specifically, we're talking about how we partied back then. Whatever the age," Caitlin responded.

Andrew gave her a long, hungry look, "Please don't be offended, but you might not have as many years to go back as some of us older folks here—"

"Like Marcus," Nelson joked. Everyone laughed while Marcus turned a shade of red made even more brilliant in the firelight.

"Fuck you, dude," Marcus muttered, as he sipped his wine.

Caitlin tossed back her golden curls and smiled mischievously, "Don't be fooled. I am older than I look."

This silenced all the men while Charmaine, Caitlin, and Lindsay smiled at each other conspiratorially.

Andrew, Marcus, and Nelson looked around nervously.

"Oooh-kay. Guess that's sorted," Andrew said sheepishly.

Nelson had forgotten that Andrew was originally from England, which meant most of the time all the straight women at any party were interested in him because of that damned accent. For the life of him, Nelson could never understand why he worked so hard at disguising it.

If it was him, he'd be using that accent every chance he got. At times he wondered if he could pick up a slight one by going to England for a while—on business of course. Caitlin's next comment snapped him out of his reverie.

"So, what *did* everyone do when they went to parties at say…fourteen?"

Marcus sighed, "Same thing I do now: eat and drink, only it was soda then—"

"No, for fun!" she responded.

"That was fun for me," he said, as he drained his glass and refilled it.

Charmaine added, "You mean like what we were talking about the 'being present and having fun' thing at that age?"

Marcus responded immediately, "Cake! I always wanted to know what kind of cake there was. I was a heavy kid. Shut up Nelson."

"What?" Nelson feigned innocence.

"Cause I just hear it buzzing around in your head—'ya still are'!"

"I would never. Man, I get a bad rep around here just cause I make a few jokes. Sheesh."

Lindsay looked at Nelson over the rim of her wine glass before draining it. "Is that what you did as a kid for fun, crack jokes all the time?"

Andrew muttered, "Yeah... it's always fun until someone puts an—what's that American saying?"

He was met with a chorus of responses from the group of "Puts an eye out!" They all giggled and laughed.... like children.

Nelson noticed Caitlin's lips again as she laughed. They *were* like pillows, soft, full, suckable pillows. He wondered what it would be like to press his mouth to hers. Then he looked into her eyes and she smiled at him. Finally! He didn't blush, nor did he look away. He took her in fully, deeply, in totality while the flames were coloring her all shades of gold. That's when he got the idea, a brilliant idea. He knew his timing was perfect because Charmaine had just poured the last drops out of one of the wine bottles as Lindsay rose to get another to replace it.

"Well... if you really want to know what I remember..." He purposely took his time. He wanted them to really want to know. "Ah, never mind."

"Aw c'mon now. Don't be a tease, what?" Andrew scolded him.

"Yeah, I am dying to know. What did you do at fourteen? Probably ran around at parties tying everyone's shoelaces together or some kind of 'joke' thing, right?" Marcus asked sarcastically.

Lindsay interrupted, "C'mon y'all, give him a break. Talk about haters!"

"It's okay Lins." Nelson said quietly. He looked over at Caitlin. She licked her lips and he noticed her chest rise and fall, as she looked at him. He knew that breath was for him. Timing. "Actually, I'm kind of ashamed to say—"

"See? I told you he did bad things to people. You were THAT kid weren't you?" Marcus said accusingly.

"Marcus, dude what's up?" Charmaine looked at him. "Have another glass of wine and chill. We're just talking."

Caitlin's spoke up. There was just a touch of huskiness to her voice and a look in her eyes that was so deep, as if she were saying all kinds of things to him without saying the words. "Guys let the man speak. I am…. intrigued."

Andrew laughed softly, "Intrigued. Indeed. Speak Nelson, you have our undivided attention."

Nelson thought, "I can make this happen, right here, right now. I've been watching, listening. The timing is perfect, and now to follow-through."

"When I was, you know, like fourteen or so, and me and my friends were at parties together—I don't know, it's like we were all just trying to figure out… things. You know?" He paused for dramatic effect.

"What things Nelson? I'm all ears." It was Caitlin egging him on, she even leaned forward towards him.

"Well you know… we…" he paused and cleared his throat because this was THE moment. The moment where you land the deal, get the apartment, get the girl, get the prize, but you had to handle it just right.

"Really? You're all shy now?" That was Charmaine, "I've known you for years and have never seen you all tongue tied--"

Marcus chimed in, "She's right! Out with it, man."

"Okay, okay, I just feel silly is all. But, if you really want to know we played all those stupid games kids play when they're all shy and you know figuring... things out--"

Lindsay roared with laughter. "Oh my God! You're talking about *those* games?!" She held up the empty wine bottle and laughed again.

Everybody else around the fire joined in the laughter and Nelson felt himself blush. Well, this wasn't turning out as he'd expected. He hated being laughed at. Then again, he had opened himself up for this—so fine. No harm, no foul. He'd figure out a stupid comeback, laugh with them, then take his leave gracefully. He'd had to risk it. Then he began to wonder if it wasn't as bad as he thought, especially since he noticed Caitlin sitting back in the chair with a different look on her face as she focused on him.

She silenced the group with one statement, "Okay. I'm game."

Marcus almost choked on his wine, "What? Game for what? What are you saying? What is she saying?" he frantically looked around the group with an expression of terror.

Caitlin picked up an empty bottle that was sitting on the table and laid it on its side atop the smooth glass surrounding the firepit. Marcus buried his head in his hands. Nelson sat up straighter and Andrew raised his eyebrows, while smiling a half smile as he looked at Caitlin.

She continued, "We were all just bitching about the fact that we spend our time not being fully engaged—even when we're at a social event. What better way to be present, you know? I mean we were talking about the good old days"

Marcus muttered, "I never said they were good. There was... there was just cake and I like cake."

Lindsay leaned forward staring at Nelson, "You want to play Spin The Bottle?"

Nelson protested, "I NEVER said that. You guys wanted to know what I did, and I told you. That's all."

Andrew sipped more wine. "Interesting."

Charmaine looked at him in disbelief, "Well, some of us are married, you know? You don't just go playing spin the bottle when you're an adult—"

"I don't know. Why not?" Lindsay interrupted her.

"Why not?" Charmaine turned to face her wife, "Are you nuts?

"What?" Lindsay said calmly slurring only one of the words. "Look, I know I'm committed to you and this isn't going to lead to anything—I KNOW that. Unless, you're not that confident in our relationship after all these years-"

"That has nothing to do with anything! First of all, I am forty years old-"

Marcus looked at Nelson, "Now you've done it—"

"Again," Nelson protested, "I've haven't done anything—it was her idea," he said, pointing at Caitlin.

Caitlin laughed. "Wow, it's just a game. And this is exactly how we know that we are a bunch of old fuddy-duddies. IT. IS. A. GAME. PEOPLE. I don't plan on going home with anyone tonight."

Nelson thought, "Not yet. We'll see."

Caitlin took a sip of wine and settled back in her chair, "Look, we don't have to do it. It just sounded like an interesting… challenge."

Charmaine almost shouted, "How is playing Spin-the-Bottle a

challenge? I am happily married, comfortable and secure in my relationship."

Andrew grinned, "Then what've you got to lose?"

Lindsay sat forward as she slapped her knee and pointed, "I'm in!" Charmaine frowned and gave her the evil eye, "Aw for fucksakes Char—it's a stupid game. Hey, lookit--this is the closest we're ever going to get to messin' around beyond 'vanilla sex 'and I'd say it's pretty harmless. There is nobody here I'm thinking about screwing tonight—no offense"

There was a chorus response of "none taken."

"Alright, I'm in," said Andrew and took a big gulp of his wine. "Uhh, so…how do you play it here in the states?"

After Caitlin explained the rules to him. There was silence as everyone looked at Charmaine.

Nelson whispered to her, "Hey, I bet this isn't something you'd thought you'd do on your fortieth birthday, huh?"

She glared at him and then looked around the circle.

Andrew began chanting, "Peer pressure, peer pressure," and

after a moment everyone joined in while laughing.

Charmaine joined in the laughter and shook her head, "Alright you fuckers, you better not ever tell anyone we did this at my party. You hear me? Honestly, I hate this game, I always lose."

As she looked around at the six people sitting around the firepit, which was slowly dying out, Lindsay said, "Look, I'm drunk enough to kiss any one of y'all. But, let it be known, I'm only sleeping with my wife."

She and Char kissed each other, which elicited a chorus of "Awwws" from the group.

"What the hell?" Marcus said and picked up the bottle. "Might as well get it over with. I'm not kissing one of you dudes though. I am secure in my sexuality, but you know… it's just… you know—it's, it's just, not happening," he sputtered.

Lindsay playfully tapped him on the shoulder as everyone laughed. He spun the bottle and then there was silence as they watched it turn.

Spinning, spinning, endlessly spinning.

"One round only, okay? I'm not playing kiddie games all night long with you guys," Char said nervously, as the bottle continued to spin.

Nelson was holding his breath. He had only one round. He had only one chance—maybe two--if Caitlin's spin stopped on him.

The bottle stopped. Right between Char and Lindsay.

"See?!" Marcus exclaimed as he began to stand. "I hate this stupid game. I never get lucky—is there any birthday cake left?"

Andrew grabbed his sleeve, "Oh no you don't. You've got to see if someone spins to you. You may just luck out on that spin buddy." He nodded towards Caitlin.

That's when Nelson realized that all the guys and maybe even Lindsay and Char were hoping to land a spin on Caitlin. This could backfire on him so badly. He hadn't clearly thought this through. He blamed it on the wine.

Sheepishly, Marcus asked, "Well, can I at least get another spin since it didn't land on anyone?"

"Nope. One spin, one round." Char was adamant. "That's how

we old folks play it tonight."

"I hope there's some fucking cake left," Marcus muttered sitting back in his chair pouting.

Lindsay reached for bottle. Charmaine began to nervously fiddle with her hair. Lindsay stopped and looked at Charmaine, "Hey babe, if you really don't—"

"Oh no, I'm not going to be the—the, buzzkill old lady tonight. Like you said, it doesn't mean anything. It's just a kiss. Go ahead."

Lindsay spun the bottle and it landed on Andrew, who grinned from ear to ear. Everyone whooped and laughed, and then it was absolute silence as Andrew and Lindsay looked at each other. Nelson noticed a few people from the other tables had come to stand around and silently watch.

"Well, here we go." Lindsay said. She reached over and squeezed Charmaine's hand.

Andrew looked around at everyone, "God, this is fucking awkward."

Lindsay deadpanned, "Thanks."

"Oh no, not you darlin' it's just. I suddenly remember how awkward this game was even back then—"

"See?! I'm not the only one," Marcus said while looking at Nelson. "And he's one of the hot ones."

"Thanks mate," Andrew said.

Lindsay had an odd look on her face as she leaned into Andrew, "Alright, y'all. I'm going in."

Andrew closed his eyes.

The air around the circle seemed to thicken as everyone held their breath. The kiss didn't last very long, but it was long enough. People began to sneak looks from the kissing couple back to Charmaine as she watched Andrew and Lindsay. Nelson was worried about how she would respond. This could be bad; it would've been better if another person had been the one Andrew had to kiss. Especially since it was the first kiss. Charmaine could get angry and end it all right now. He watched as her features seemed to morph into something he couldn't read. When they finally stopped, Andrew and Lindsay looked at each other for a long moment. Then Lindsay shyly looked back at Charmaine.

"Okay. Okay," Charmaine said, as she took a long drink of wine, and everyone seemed to tense, afraid of having caused Charmain pain on her birthday.

As the silence continued, Nelson noticed Andrew looking everywhere but within the circle, while Lindsay's eyes were glued to Charmaine. Her eyes began to mist over as she tightly held onto Charmaine's hand.

"That was….Fucking….HOT!!" Charmaine exclaimed. "Wow, I kinda… I didn't expect that it would… you know… " She wrapped her arms around Lindsay. "Oh baby."

"You're not mad?" Lindsay asked her softly, while her face was buried in her hair.

"Naw, kind of—" and she whispered something into Lindsay's ear that sent them both into peals of laughter, which caused everyone else to join in, although for Nelson it was nervous laughter.

Caitlin spoke over the laughter, "Hey Andrew, your turn."

"Okay," he said with a sigh.

He spun the bottle and it turned and turned finally landing on

Marcus.

"Aw crap," Marcus muttered. "Nope, not doing it."

"Why not? You might like it," That was Charmaine, grinning

mischievously.

"Cause I told you that is a non-negotiable."

Charmaine growled out, "C'mon, you might like it."

Geneva laughed, "Oh my God, we have created a monster."

"Hey just give him a peck on the cheek." Nelson egged him on.

"Not like I really want to kiss you either. Not really my speed,"

Andrew said. "Okay? So, I'll forfeit."

"Not fair. Just peck him on the cheek, c'mon it's the twenty-first

century, Marcus. You never know; you might like it." Caitlin said smiling.

"Uhh, no I won't" Marcus said firmly.

Lindsay, seeming offended for a moment said, "You're really

adamant there Marcus—what's going on? Something you've got issues

with that--"

"No! Okay, look I've tried it once and it wasn't for me."

Which elicited whoops, laughter, and a myriad of comments as

Marcus turned red yet again.

"Alright! Alright!" He leaned over and planted a quick peck on Andrew's lips. "There. Satisfied? I'm going to get some goddamned cake," he said as he stormed off.

The silence that followed was tense until Andrew said, "Worst date ever."

Everyone laughed again as Charmaine refilled wine glasses.

Andrew looked around the group, "Shall we keep going?"

"Why not? I want my turn," Charmaine said to everyone's surprise.

Caitlin reached forward for the bottle, "Since he's gone, guess I'll spin. Anybody mind?"

Nelson realized that his palms were sweating, and his stomach was doing weird shit. "What the hell?" he thought. So what? If she landed on him, big deal it's one kiss. Then it became clear that if it didn't land on him, then he only had one more chance. He began to calculate what he would do if that were the case. He started planning how he would remedy the situation if it didn't land on him... how he would maneuver everything to--

The whoops and laughter around him brought him out of his reverie. He looked at the table and saw that Caitlin's spin had landed on Geneva, who was now beet red--and it wasn't from the fire pit.

"You okay with this?" Caitlin was asking Geneva.

Geneva looked around and took a deep breath, "Why not?" she said as Caitlin stood to what looked to be a full five feet eleven inches of height. Geneva rose to meet her, although she was about five foot one. She looked like a child next to Caitlin. Geneva's knee began to nervously bounce so she looked as though she had to pee.

Andrew started and soon the whole group was chanting, "Go Geneva! Go Geneva! Go Geneva!"

Charmaine shouted, "You've got this!"

Geneva's hands were nervously twisting the end of her sweater. Caitlin gently took her hands in hers and held them. She tenderly bent her face towards Geneva, while moving one hand to her chin. She lifted her face and lightly kissed her lips, then their mouths came together for a moment as Geneva closed her eyes. It lasted less than a minute.

Geneva raised her hands in victory. Caitlin smiled at her and returned to her seat.

"See? It was kind of fun, wasn't it?" asked Lindsay.

Geneva stuttered, "I was—you know—I don't usually—"

"Kiss girls?" Charmaine finished for her.

"No, I never have! But that wasn't it—I just... you know—it's been a while. I mean, yeah that was different, but it was—you know it was okay—I mean, better than okay, nice—really nice--but I just I haven't been with any—it's not just that she's a girl—I- I mean--I don't do—"

Andrew whispered to Nelson, "Holy shit, I think she's a virgin."

Nelson immediately felt bad that he'd foisted this stupid game on everyone so he could have a chance to kiss Caitlin. Especially now since he only had one chance left.

"I heard that Andrew and I am NOT!" Geneva looked at him angrily, "I'm just not into--PDA, you know? Besides, we don't know each other and—and--yeah, okay—I am a little bit old fashioned about wanting to know someone I make out with! Okay? So what? You know?

Just--" She grabbed a half full bottle of wine, poured another glass, and downed it.

"What'd I miss!?" Marcus came into the circle with a plate of half-eaten cake. He had frosting smeared on his face causing people to snicker at him.

"What?" He looked around at everyone. "What's so funny?"

Charmaine was laughing so hard she was almost in tears, "Oh my God, this is the best birthday party ever! "As she gasped for breath, she looked at Geneva sitting in the chair with her head down, staring into her wine glass, and her mood sobered as best it could under the situation. "Geneva, I'm not sure you want to do this, but baby it's your spin. Do you want to forfeit?"

Geneva sat up, placed the wine glass on the table and looked around the circle before saying, "Hell naw, bitches. I've got this." This sent everyone back into gales of laughter.

Geneva grasped the bottle and spun it hard. It was so hard it almost fell off the table. Everyone was watching the bottle, mesmerized. Nelson was hoping it wouldn't stop on him, but then again, hey, at least he'd get to kiss someone tonight.

"Damn, it's really like I'm fifteen again. Freaking out, hoping someone—anyone picks me," he thought.

He looked around the table and everyone was watching the spinning bottle with great anticipation.

Finally, it stopped.

The bottle was pointed at... Marcus who was standing directly in the line of the opening, still holding his plate with bits of birthday cake remaining.

There was a chorus of, "Ooo". Marcus's eyes looked as if they would pop out of his head.

"What? Really—" he said.

He didn't get to finish what he was saying because in one smooth move, Geneva had taken the plate from his hands, throwing it behind her so that it landed across the yard, and grabbed Marcus's face planting a kiss on his lips. But, it wasn't just any kind of kiss, it was deep. From where he was sitting Nelson--and everyone else—could see there was serious tongue action from both of them. They were locked together for what seemed like five minutes all the while there were side comments from the group.

Andrew exclaimed, "Damn!" around minute two.

Lindsay's eyebrows rose, "Jesus—uhm—uhm—uhm…."

Charmaine cheered them on at minute four, "Go on now!! Whew!"

Caitlin's eyes burned intensely as she said, "Now THAT is a kiss people!"

By then Marcus's arms were around Geneva's waist and she was holding onto his shoulders.

Nelson was left speechless. How could Marcus, dweeby, schlubby Marcus, be giving the best kiss of the night? He had to admit, it was a team effort on their part. Nelson was impressed.

The kiss ended sweetly, with Geneva and Marcus kissing each other's cheeks and briefly holding hands. Witnessing this there was a smattering of "Awwws," from the group. As Geneva returned to her seat, Marcus whispered to no one in particular, "I won. I finally won." Geneva smiled shyly at him.

There was silence as everyone realized what they'd just witnessed. Lindsay popped the cork on some Prosecco and brought everyone out of their reverie about the moment. It almost seemed crude to continue with the game, but Charmaine looked at Nelson.

"Okay Nels, this was your bright idea. Spin it buddy!"

Nelson wanted to forfeit. After all, how could he top that? It was better that the evening end on a sweet tender note. Big deal, he wouldn't have his chance to kiss Caitlin. He would ask her for her phone number. They'd have this evening to talk and laugh over if she agreed to go out with him. But, what if she said no? What if he backed out and he lost the hard-won respect he seemed to have gained from her? He felt torn about what to do.

"We're waiting." It was Caitlin speaking to him.

She was sitting in the chair, her legs folded beneath her again. She looked like a queen ruling her universe. There was a slight autumn wind blowing, it wasn't cold, but it moved the air and her hair was billowing softly in the wind. What was left of the fire gave her an otherworldly glow. The look she gave him was an invitation as if she'd understood his motives all along. He wondered if anyone else had picked

up on that look.

Nelson cleared his throat and took a sip of the freshly poured

prosecco. This was it. The thing--the follow through--and he was

prepared. He was ready. Now all he needed was luck, and yes, timing so

that the bottle stopped on Caitlin. He changed his mind; *this* would be

the perfect way to end the night. He imagined what it would feel like to

kiss those lips and... Maybe this would be the beginning of something

they would finish later tonight.

"C'mon lady luck, let me have this one thing tonight," he thought

as he laid his hand on the bottle and spun it. He didn't want to look at it.

He couldn't bear it if it landed on someone else, and no, he was not

going to kiss Marcus or Andrew. He was drunk, but he wanted one thing

and one thing only: those lips. Nelson had a plan, if it landed on someone

else he'd "accidentally" knock it over, ending the game with a laugh

about being a klutz. Fine with him.

It just kept spinning. It was making him crazy.

At last, it stopped. Nelson looked down at the bottle and slowly let his eyes trace the path to the other side.

IT WAS HER!

It took everything he had within him not to get up and do a 'happy dance.' That would not be cool, but inside he was dancing his ass off.

Caitlin stood up, waiting, with a look that seemed to be throwing down a gauntlet. A challenge for him. He stood up and walked towards her. He started to feel his chest tighten. He was so excited he almost couldn't breathe. He heard someone whisper, "this is gonna be good." He thought it sounded like Charmaine.

Lindsay let out a loud, "Whoop!!" as he and Caitlin moved closer to one another.

Geneva, who was sitting in a chair with Marcus on the ground beside her, surreptitiously rubbing her leg, said, "Go Nelson, go Nelson—oh my God, this *is* like being fifteen again."

Everyone laughed.

Nelson, remembering the kiss between Marcus and Geneva, realized this one had to be even more special. He knew just what he was going to do to make it memorable--to make it special. He brushed her hair back from her face with one hand. Caitlin blushed a little bit and shyly smiled at him.

"It's like they're on a bloody date!" Andrew called out and everyone laughed again.

Nelson stepped even closer to Caitlin and gently taking her face in his hands he kissed first her upper lip, then her lower. She took a deep breath and he could swear he felt her tremble with each tiny kiss. Then he leaned in and fully kissed her on the lips. They were as soft, if not softer than he had imagined they'd be. It was all that he wanted in that moment. It was VICTORY!

But, then something in him snapped, panicked, freaked out— he couldn't name it or explain it, but he couldn't stop himself. Nelson rammed his tongue into her mouth hard. Caitlin frowned, but he didn't see her because his eyes were closed. But, he could swear he'd heard a soft "Ooooof" sound from her. What he did notice is that she began to bat his tongue around inside her mouth with her tongue. In retaliation he began to bat her tongue with his—which made Caitlin jab her tongue down his throat, almost all the way down his throat! Nelson had never kissed anyone with such a long tongue—when did it end?! Again, bat, thrust, parry—he was back in high school fencing class and she had the longer saber! He was still holding her face and she reached up and grabbed his face, holding it in an almost vise-like grip. He wanted this to stop, but it was too late, he'd gone too far. Nelson had thought that she was up for a challenge, but he hadn't meant to respond to the gauntlet while his tongue was in her mouth.

THRUST, ADVANCE, PARRY—JAB, PARRY, THRUST

Nelson began trying to use his tongue to push hers out of his mouth out so he could let go. It wasn't working. Every move he made with his, she countered, and he was stuck in this purgatory of entwined tongues.

There were standing by the firepit, holding each other's faces, pushing their tongues all over each other's mouths.

That's when he began to wonder "*Who's idea was this anyway?! How did I end up here?*" He realized, "Shit, it was mine. My really brilliant idea!"

"That is not a good look going on," Charmaine whispered to Lindsay.

Lindsay watched for a moment and said to Charmaine, "I must be really drunk--hey y'all, is it just me or does it look like they're wrestling?"

That was exactly what it felt like to Nelson! From fencing to wrestling. It was as if they were trying to pin each other's tongues down. There was saliva running down his chin. He was trying to get air through his nose, because he couldn't get any in his mouth since it was glued to Caitlin's.

"That's the dodgiest kiss I've ever seen," observed Andrew. He shouted at them, "Doesn't that hurt mate?"

"Yeah, you know... I can't watch this," Marcus said, as he took Geneva's hand in his and stood to leave, "

"This is really, you know, like—disturbing," Geneva shuddered, as she rinsed her mouth with wine and swallowed, leaving the circle.

Caitlin slipped an arm inside Nelson's right arm and began to pull on him. Nelson was wondering what had happened to the tender, gentle woman who had kissed Geneva. This felt like he imagined kissing the

Loch Ness Monster would feel like. As if Nessie were thrashing around in his mouth. He began trying to extricate himself from Caitlin. She pushed her tongue all the way down his throat again and he thought he might just die, right there, because there was no air.

"Okay! Okay you two—" That was Lindsay. "Y'all are ruining it!"

Charmaine stood up, "My birthday party is being ruined Nels—Lindsay I'm going inside. This is too much—"

"It's bollocks is what it is!" Andrew was disgusted as he grabbed his glass and left the circle. "Just fucking bollocks!"

By now there was saliva running down Nelson and Caitlin's neckline. He was making little grunting sounds as they continued to tongue wrestle. All he could think was, "MAKE IT STOP!! Dear God! Please make this stop!!!"

Charmaine looked at them, which neither of them saw, and shouted, "I'M DONE!! You hear me?! You two, just—oh God..." She left the circle.

As she began to leave Lindsay leaned into the kissing-tussling couple, "What a way to ruin my wife's birthday. Asshat!" And she stormed off.

The rest of the circle diminished as well, leaving Nelson and Caitlin with arms, lips, and tongues locked into each other.

Finally, Nelson was able to get leverage by shifting himself behind one of the chairs so that their bodies were on opposite sides and then he pushed as hard as he could. Once separated they were both still standing. His tongue hurt. The muscles in his face hurt. He kept the chair between them as he and Caitlin silently looked at each other. He was speechless. He was trying to figure out where he had gone wrong— observe, okay, he'd done that. Listen, he'd done that, and heard the huskiness in her voice and the willingness in her words. The timing was perfect, the bottle *had* landed on her—it was in the follow through. He'd left the bench without both sneakers. He couldn't figure out what had snapped inside him. Why had he panicked?

He looked at Caitlin. She had saliva on her face and shirt, her eyes were intense, almost glowing. Her hair was a mess. Her clothes were rumpled, and she was breathing heavily, just like he was. Nelson picked up the bottle of prosecco and drank out of it, a long cleansing pull, then silently passed it to her. After she took a long drink, she wiped her mouth and glared at him. They could hear the crickets in the yard chirping away. There were a few sounds coming from inside the house. Not everyone had left the party yet. A gentle breeze ruffled through their clothing.

They stood there for a few minutes, which seemed like an hour to Nelson, while they both looked everywhere but at each other. He replayed it in his mind. What the hell had happened? He began to wonder if, in his panic, he had thrown down a challenge to her because he wanted to see what would happen. That made sense to him. Sort of anyway. Maybe not. He didn't know. He didn't know what he should do, which was a first. He wasn't angry. He didn't know how or what he was feeling. So, he just stood there and took another long drink from the bottle.

Caitlin brushed her hair out of her face and turned to face him, "So... what? You wanna go again?"

Nelson paused as he understood that during that kiss he'd never been more present to anything in life. He realized that this was a first for him. He was surprised when a slow smile spread across his face, as

he said. "Give me a minute."

FINAL THOUGHTS ON KISSING.…

I just love kissing. I would be happy to make out with a guy for hours and it doesn't have to necessarily lead to anything. (CAT)

I just think, that however we came to kissing as a species I think it ranks right up there with the opposable thumb, or our ability to reason because the kiss separates us from a lot of other species. In that we kiss for connection. All kisses aren't sexual. Cause if you see other species kiss, it's going to lead to something sexual. It's going to lead to something else when they connect but we as human beings make a lot of decisions and make a lot of meaning from a kiss.

It's almost like there's a lost art to kissing. Maybe because the times don't feel as tender, maybe everybody is trying to rush to something else. What happened? Does the art of kissing change with the times? Our music is less tender. Love songs are about betrayal or getting it on. I grew up in a time when you prided yourself on your ability to really love somebody or to really bring it to somebody in a way that was unforgettable. Whether you wanted to be with them or have a great sexual experience it was about paying attention to these things. That's how we were indoctrinated because the love movement was really important. I don't think that the times now lead to us thinking that way. (DC)

It's always the first kiss [that] is always so interesting. The anticipation of are we going to kiss or not kiss. I am wondering if I'm sending out my "don't kiss me" vibe. I've never initiated a first kiss. I think it's my Christian background. Girls don't do that. (CR)

I think it doesn't have to be on the lips. I think a kiss at the right moment is like someone wrapping their arms you and saying I'll never let go. (VB)

Cocktails for Kissers
(With all of these, adjust to taste— just like a kiss)

FIRST KISS:
2 oz. of whiskey
2 oz. of Chambord
3 oz. of simple syrup
A squeeze of lemon juice to taste
Mix in a cocktail shaker, pour over ice and garnish with a lemon slice

THE FRENCH KISS:
2 oz. of limoncello
1 oz. of vanilla vodka
3-4 oz of prosecco
Muddled raspberries
Mix limoncello and vanilla vodka in a shaker with ice. Place muddled raspberries in the bottom of a cocktail glass, then add the prosecco

BEST KISS:

2 oz. Vanilla vodka

2 oz. Raspberry vodka

1 oz. Coconut liqueur (or rum)

1 oz. Irish Cream liqueur

Mix all the ingredients in cocktail shaker with ice, serve over ice.

Optional: garnish with chocolate shavings

About the Author

Born in Louisville, KY, Renee´ currently makes her home in New York City. This is Renee´s first foray into writing short stories in MANY years. As a playwright she has written over sixty short (10 minute- to one- act) plays, numerous full-length plays and four screenplays. Her most recent is the award- winning short film, *The Brotherhood.* Renee´ is also a singer-songwriter, actor and a teaching artist.

www.ingramcontent.com/pod-product-compliance
Lightning Source LLC
Chambersburg PA
CBHW021141130626
46554CB00005B/1616

* 9 7 8 0 5 7 8 6 5 3 5 6 3 *